V

Man, Nurse Meehan cleaned up good.

In all his years in the army, Cal had never gotten
used to the way some women could pull that off—
looking one way all the time until you more or
less forgot they were even female—and then doing
whatever it was they did to end up looking like *this*.

Meehan was wearing a dress. He'd never seen her
in a dress. It was colorful, flowery, kind of floaty
and thin.

Her shoulders were bare, except for the little straps,
and soft looking, smooth, touchable. He could
imagine how good they'd feel if he ran his hands
over them.

Don't go there! he thought.

One of the little straps dropped off her shoulder.

Take it easy, Cal!

This was Nurse Meehan here—and he was acting as
if she was a real woman or something....

D0186897

Dear Reader,

Instead of writing your resolutions, I have the perfect way to begin the new year—read this month's spectacular selection of Silhouette Special Edition romances! These exciting books will put a song in your heart, starting with another installment of our very popular MONTANA MAVERICKS series—*In Love With Her Boss* by the stellar Christie Ridgway. Christie vows this year to "appreciate the time I have with my husband and sons and appreciate *them* for the unique people they are."

Lindsay McKenna brings us a thrilling story from her MORGAN'S MERCENARIES: DESTINY'S WOMEN series with *Woman of Innocence*, in which an adventure-seeking beauty meets up with the legendary—and breathtaking—mercenary of her dreams! The excitement continues with Victoria Pade's next tale, *On Pins and Needles*, in her A RANCHING FAMILY series. Here, a skeptical sheriff falls for a lovely acupuncturist who finds the wonder cure for all his doubts—her love!

And what does a small-town schoolteacher do when she finds a baby on her doorstep? Find out in Nikki Benjamin's heartwarming reunion romance *Rookie Cop*. A love story you're sure to savor is *The Older Woman* by Cheryl Reavis, in which a paratrooper captain falls head over heels for the tough-talking nurse living next door. This year, Cheryl wants to "stop and smell the roses." I also recommend Lisette Belisle's latest marriage-of-convenience story, *The Wedding Bargain*, in which an inheritance—and two hearts—are at stake! Lisette believes that the new year means "a fresh start, and vows to meet each new day with renewed faith, energy and a sense of humor."

I'm pleased to celebrate with you the beginning of a brand-new year. May you also stop to smell the roses, and find many treasures in Silhouette Special Edition the whole year through!

Enjoy!

Karen Taylor Richman
Senior Editor

Please address questions and book requests to:
Silhouette Reader Service
U.S.: 3010 Walden Ave., P.O. Box 1325, Buffalo, NY 14269
Canadian: P.O. Box 609, Fort Erie, Ont. L2A 5X3

The Older Woman

CHERYL REAVIS

Silhouette®

SPECIAL EDITION™

Published by Silhouette Books

America's Publisher of Contemporary Romance

In memory of Milly,
the only pogo cello player I've ever known
and the best, one-nurse sales force
a romance writer ever had. Miss you, girl!

SILHOUETTE BOOKS

ISBN 0-373-24445-2

THE OLDER WOMAN

This edition published by arrangement with Harlequin Books S.A.

® and TM are trademarks of Harlequin Books S.A., used under license.
Trademarks indicated with ® are registered in the United States Patent
and Trademark Office, the Canadian Trade Marks Office and in other
countries.

Visit Silhouette at www.eHarlequin.com

Printed in U.S.A.

CHERYL REAVIS,

award-winning short-story author and romance novelist who also writes under the name of Cinda Richards, describes herself as a "late bloomer" who played in her first piano recital at the tender age of thirty. "We had to line up by height—I was the third smallest kid," she says. "After that, there was no stopping me. I immediately gave myself permission to attempt my *other* heart's desire—to write." Her Silhouette Special Edition novel *A Crime of the Heart* reached millions of readers in *Good Housekeeping* magazine. Both *A Crime of the Heart* and *Patrick Gallagher's Widow* won the Romance Writers of America's coveted RITA Award for Best Contemporary Series Romance the year they were published. *One of Our Own* received the Career Achievement Award for Best Innovative Series Romance from *Romantic Times Magazine*. A former public health nurse, Cheryl makes her home in North Carolina with her husband.

Dear Reader,

Writers are often asked where they get their ideas. The best answer I've heard to this question is that we don't get ideas—ideas get us. That was very much the case regarding *The Older Woman*.

Naturally, as a romance writer, I was already interested in creating stories about love conquering all, but this time I wanted a somewhat different approach. I wanted to do a "hero's journey." I have long since learned that heroes are where you find them—sometimes in the most unlikely places and often in a supporting role in a previous book. They are "ideas" that appear from out of nowhere, plant themselves firmly in a writer's creative process and refuse to go away.

I knew early on that Calvin "Bugs" Doyle had the makings of the kind of hero I wanted to write about. I also knew that just any woman wouldn't do for him. If his journey was to be truly arduous, then there had to be serious obstacles to their relationship. It wasn't enough for her to be "unattainable" because of the difference in their ages. She had to be as heroic as he was. She had to have made her own journey, so that she could understand his fears on a very personal level. She had to be every bit the survivor that he was.

I admire survivors. I believe in love. And I'm happiest when I'm telling the story of two people who couldn't be more mismatched, but who find in each other more than they ever dared hope.

My hope is that you will enjoy *The Older Woman*.

Sincerely,

Cheryl Reavis

Chapter One

"Happy is the bride the sun shines on."

Specialist 4 Calvin "Bugs" Doyle sat staring out the second-story window. There had been no sun today, and it was still raining, a relentless kind of drumming on the roof that left him no room for anything but feeling sorry for himself.

The melancholy had come down on him all at once and without warning. He hadn't expected it. He'd been significantly discouraged for weeks, of course. Months, even—but it was nothing compared to the sadness he was feeling now. Man, did he want to go somewhere and cry in his beer. If he'd been able, he would have been in some off-limits dive right this minute, knocking back a few and wallowing in the whiny lyrics of a good old country-western song. And when he had enough of a buzz on, no doubt he would have joined right in, singing his sorry heart out—probably over the very vocal protests of his fellow patrons until he eventually got tossed out the door.

It wasn't as if he didn't know the wedding was going to happen. What with the bride's misgivings and the groom's perpetual physical rehabilitation, the actual ceremony had been a long time coming. So long that he'd been recruited to help plan the damned thing. The problem here wasn't that he was uninformed. The *problem* was did he or didn't he still have it bad for Rita Warren?

He must, he finally decided, because he'd made the considerable effort it took to get himself to the church, just so he could watch her get married to another man. He must, because he'd made a point of not saying or doing anything stupid the whole time he was there. He must, because the bottom line here was that he really did want her to be happy. And wasn't that a hell of a note? He'd seen Rita through thick and thin—mostly thin. If anybody deserved a little sunshine on her back door, it was Rita. Even he realized that.

He smiled slightly to himself.

Rita, Rita, he thought, shaking his head. There is nobody like you, girl.

He had at least managed to give her a chaste goodbye-and-good-luck kiss—albeit under the watchful eye of his superior officer and, as it happened, her new husband. Lieutenant McGraw was one more lucky bastard. He'd survived a Black Hawk helicopter crash and he'd gotten the girl, while he, Calvin "Bugs" Doyle, the only other survivor of the same crash, remained, simply and always, said girl's "friend."

He took a quiet breath.

Get yourself together here, Doyle.

He had always known the rules of engagement. There was absolutely no reason for him to feel so down about this thing. He understood the situation. Rita had never for one minute led him on. She had always been straight with him, even when she'd been so abandoned and penniless she'd had to move in with him for a while. She had lived with him— on her terms—and she had been grateful for his help. But she didn't love him, not like that, not the way he had wanted.

Just friends.

No. *Best* friends. He knew everything there was to know about Rita Warren. Everything. The good and the bad, and it hadn't mattered to him. Unfortunately, what he knew hadn't mattered to her, either. It was the lieutenant's knowing she'd worried about.

But it had turned out all right for her, and he supposed, when everything was said and done, being a friend was better than nothing.

He closed his eyes and tried not to think about

how beautiful Rita had looked today. He didn't want
to think about the honeymoon, either. He was so
tired, and his legs were beginning to hurt. If he
didn't get up and walk around soon, he'd regret it.
He had mistakenly believed that finally getting both
of the leg casts off would make the pain situation
better. Wrong. No casts just meant that the muscles
in his legs had to work harder. Which meant more
pain.

The wind shifted, and the rain beat against the
windows.

"Happy is the bride the sun shines on."

The truth was this bride had been happy without
the sun—without much of anything, if you got right
down to it. The groom's parents hadn't exactly
given their blessing, and Rita didn't get much in the
way of a family send-off—unless you counted her
little girl, Olivia. Olivia had a ball getting all dressed
up and blowing kisses and scattering rose petals. Except for Olivia, Rita didn't have any relatives she or
anybody else would want to claim. The closest thing
to a bona fide well-wisher she had was good old
"Bugs" Doyle—and he could have gone either
way. Even so, he had still dragged himself to the
wedding.

Just for her.

A sudden sharp pain made him jerk his legs to try
to get away from it. The cane he needed for walking
slid off the nearby straight chair and clattered to the
floor. He swore under his breath, but he made no

effort to get it. He stared out the window again, breathing deeply they way he'd been taught, trying to fight down the intense burning ache before it got the best of him.

But the pain wasn't going away. He had to get up and shuffle around, and he had to do it now. It didn't make a whole lot of sense to him that the way to make the hurting less was to do everything he could to make it hurt more, but that seemed to be the way of things. He *was* walking again—and what were the odds of that, given the degree of his injuries and the ups and downs of his prolonged recovery? He was a work in progress, all right. His only comfort was the fact that Lieutenant McGraw had made it all the way back—pain or no pain. And so would "Bugs" Doyle.

He couldn't see the cane, much less reach it. He was too tall to be comfortable in a chair low enough to pick up anything he dropped on the floor, anyway. He was going to have to get up—and then get down. And then get back up again. Deep knee bends on legs that had already had one hell of a workout today. If he was lucky, he might finish with this little project by sundown.

It was going to be struggle enough just to push himself out of the chair, but he wasn't even tempted by the option of yelling for his landlady. The word *can't* had been weeded out of his vocabulary years ago in basic training. He had no doubt that little old Mrs. Bee would come help him out here—if he asked—except she probably wasn't any better at deep knee bends than he was.

Nice old lady, Mrs. Bee. Kate Meehan, one of the nurses at the hospital had arranged for him to move into an upstairs apartment in Mrs. Bee's house after the doctors finally promoted him to an outpatient. He had no place else he wanted to go. He'd given up the trailer he had shared briefly with Rita, even before he and the lieutenant had ridden the Black Hawk into the ground, and he just wasn't up to living with a bunch of other soldiers who would feel sorry for him whether they said so or not. He knew the army would keep him on if he wanted, make room for him somewhere—if he could come back far enough. But he didn't want an audience of his peers on hand for the trip, and he figured somehow Meehan knew that.

The apartment was fairly close to the post hospital, and it was cheap enough for an enlisted man to afford. Meehan had warned him up front that Mrs. Bee's house was smoke and alcohol free, and that he would absolutely have to promise he'd ''behave,'' if he wanted her to vouch for him.

Like he could do anything else. His days of dancing naked with a rose in his teeth were pretty much behind him. His hands were more or less working again and didn't look too bad, but he couldn't half get around. Regardless of what his old drill sergeant always said, it wasn't entirely true that where there was a will there was a way. Actually, he would have liked to have raised a little hell, even before the incentive of Rita's wedding, but the best he could do for recreation these days was to eat, sleep and, with a great deal of effort, strum a little guitar.

Behave? No problem. Too easy.

So now he had a combination living room, dining room, kitchenette and one bedroom on the back side of the second floor of Mrs. Bee's big Victorian house. No cigarettes. No whiskey. No wild women. Oh, and it would be really good if he didn't swear.

So far, he and Mrs. Bee were getting along. She didn't seem to mind his so-called music, and he didn't cuss where she could hear him. Of course, he was pretty far away from her part of the house, and her hearing wasn't what it used to be.

He had his own backstairs entrance, but he was welcome to use the front door if he wanted. He'd once made the mistake of coming in the front way when Mrs. Bee and the church ladies were meeting. Talk about getting pounced on. He'd never been so clucked over in his life. One minute he was minding his own business, struggling purposefully toward the stairs, and the next minute he was sitting in the parlor with his feet up, having chocolate cake, salty peanuts, bread-and-butter pickles and some kind of cherry-cola-and-pineapple-juice punch with the "girls." It was kind of a hoot, really. He even remembered to say "please" and "thank you" and make Mrs. Bee proud. Nice old ladies—except for the one who thought anybody in the military was trash and didn't do much to hide it when Mrs. Bee was out of the room. Man, could they bake, though, even the snooty one.

But, no matter which way he came or went, he still had to drag himself up and down all kind of steps every day—the prospect of which had made his various surgeons positively beam with approval. Just what the doctors ordered, every one of them. He was okay with the on-going challenge of getting in and out of Mrs. Bee's house, and he was okay with the self-imposed "behaving." He had to be if he was ever going to make it back to where he was before the Black Hawk went down.

But first, he had to pick up the damned cane.

He managed to make it to his feet on the first try.

"Not bad," he said aloud—if he focused on the end result and not the process.

And now that he was more or less vertical, he could see into the backyard of the house next door—Meehan's house. Sometimes he could see her, too, mostly when she left for work in the mornings. Sometimes she had breakfast outside on the patio—here lately with some guy Doyle assumed was a new boyfriend, a "suit," who would arrive with a little white bag of bagels and coffee, chat her up for a little while, make her laugh, then go.

Sometimes, on her days off, Meehan fiddled around out there with plants and hanging baskets and clay pots. She apparently liked growing things—there were flowers all over the place. And wind chimes. The woman liked her wind chimes. He could hear them at night if he cut off the air conditioner and left the windows open.

Occasionally Meehan just sat on a lounge chair by herself and read. She definitely had nice legs, nice enough that it was no hardship for him to pay attention to her comings and goings. She always waved if she happened to see him in the window, but she didn't bother him. As far as he knew, she'd never checked up on him or anything like that. Apparently, his word that he'd wouldn't upset old Mrs. Bee had been good enough for her, and he appreciated that.

He hadn't seen her much the past few days, though. It kind of surprised him that she hadn't come to Rita's wedding. He knew she'd been invited, and he knew she liked Rita and Lieutenant McGraw both. In fact, Meehan was one of the few people who had openly approved of the big Warren-McGraw romance—besides him. And he did ultimately approve, regardless of the current ache in his gut. He was nothing if not a realist.

A woman either loves you or she doesn't. Period.

Doyle shifted his weight and kept watching out the window, mostly because Meehan and the boyfriend had just come out of the house. She was standing in the gravel driveway with her arms folded. She was standing—and the guy was pacing. And talking. Every now and then he gestured with both hands—a "What do you want from me?" kind of thing.

Apparently nothing, Doyle decided, because it didn't look as if Meehan answered him. She wasn't even looking at him. She just stood there with the rain beating down on her.

The boyfriend was talking again, waving his hands around a little too much, Doyle thought.

Threatening?

No. Not threatening. Or if he was, he wasn't making much of an impression. Meehan didn't seem to be intimidated by him. Still, this was *not* the Meehan he knew. He'd been a patient on her ward for months. She had a mouth on her. She was tough— tough enough to hand it out and then some if the situation called for it. And it sure looked to him as if this one required at least some kind of comeback on her part.

The boyfriend said something else, then turned and walked to his car.

Meehan stared after him, but she didn't try to stop him. He slammed the car door and drove away, accelerating too much for the weather conditions in the process and slinging mud and gravel all the way to the street.

Meehan stood for a moment after he'd gone. Doyle thought she was about to go into the house, but she didn't. Rain or no rain, she abruptly sat down on a nearby stone bench.

Was she crying?

Nah, she wasn't crying.

Well, hell, maybe she was…

Doyle abruptly pushed himself away from the window. Either way, it was all over now. The boyfriend had gone his merry way, and Meehan's current emotional state was none of his business. He had enough troubles of his own.

He held on to the furniture to maneuver to where he could get the cane. It hadn't entirely hit the floor after all. It had caught in the chair rung, and he managed to retrieve it without too much difficulty.

He stood leaning on the cane, out of breath but more than a little pleased that the retrieval hadn't turned into some kind of major production. He suddenly remembered the drama in the backyard next door and lurched over to the window again. Meehan was exactly where he'd left her.

"Damn, Meehan," he said. "How long are you going to sit there like that?"

He felt like rapping on the window pane until he got her attention, and then yelling at her to get in out of the rain—as if she was a little kid who refused to take note of the weather until somebody of authority insisted.

But he didn't rap, and he didn't yell. He moved back to the chair, fully intending to sit down. He'd had enough of the "damsel in distress" thing with Rita. As knights in shining armor went, he was pretty dented up these days. He felt no need whatsoever to go riding to the rescue. All he felt was…aggravation. He was fully aware that he owed Meehan—for telling him about the apartment in the first place and for vouching for him with Mrs. Bee so he could move in. But, damn it all, he was tired. His day had already been hell, and it wasn't even dark yet.

He sighed and looked around the room, then at the clock. It was time for Mrs. Bee's regular Sunday ritual. No matter what, Sunday afternoons were iced tea and cake time.

Well, what the hell.

He needed the exercise. He could just make a trip downstairs—and more than likely, by the time he got to the front hall, Meehan would have come to and gone inside. And then he wouldn't have to worry about it. He could stop in the kitchen and shoot the breeze with Mrs. Bee instead, hopefully talk her out of a piece of that cake with the pineapple-and-coconut-cream icing he liked so much.

He'd kill two birds with one stone—three if you counted keeping himself occupied so he wouldn't think so much about the disconcerting state of his health—four, if you threw in Rita.

Sounded like a plan to him.

It took him a while to get down the staircase. The effort made his legs hurt a lot more than he antici-pated, and he kept having to stop and get over it. He didn't see Mrs. Bee anywhere. The front door was wide open, but the screen was latched. She hadn't gone out on the porch.

He could hear the rain beating down on the gran-
ite steps outside. Mrs. Bee didn't like air-
conditioning in her part of the house, and it was hot
in the front hallway. An old brass-and-wood ceiling
fan wobbled overhead, but it was way too muggy
and humid for it to help much.

He stood for a moment at the kitchen door, then
hobbled inside to the far window. The toe of his left
shoe kept dragging on the red and white linoleum
tiles. Not a good sign. He was a lot more tired than
he thought. He finally got himself situated in front
of the window and moved the fruit-print curtain
aside so he could see out.

"Is Katie still out there?" Mrs. Bee asked behind
him.

"Yeah," he said, relieved that a little old lady
creeping up on him like that hadn't made him jump.

"It's none of our business if she wants to sit in
the rain," Mrs. Bee said, peering past his elbow.

"Right," he agreed without hesitation. His opinion exactly.

"But…"

He could feel Mrs. Bee looking at him, but he
didn't say anything. He didn't dare. It hadn't even
occurred to him that she might have been watching
out the window, too, and no way in hell was he
going to walk into a loaded opening like that.

"Calvin?" Mrs. Bee said after a moment. She
sounded every bit the schoolteacher she used to be.

Class was in session, and he had just been called on.

"No way, Mrs. Bee," he said, trying to stay ahead of her.

"Somebody really ought to do something."

"You don't mean 'somebody,' Mrs. Bee. You mean me."

"Yes, Calvin, I do. *I* can't go. It will look as if I'm meddling. If *you* go, it'll just look as if you don't know any better."

He glanced at her.

"Well, it will," she said. "Men don't know about these things—especially soldiers. It's all that hunt the hill, get the hill, way of doing things. She knows you, Calvin. She likes you. She's not going to be offended if you go."

He didn't know about any of that. All he knew was that he'd had more than one occasion to see Meehan when she was "offended," and it wasn't something he cared to repeat.

"Mrs. Bee—"

"It's just so…worrisome," she interrupted. "Katie sitting out there in the rain like that. She had that bad spell of pneumonia last winter. She ought not be out there in the wet."

"It's July, Mrs. Bee. I think she'll be all right."

"Maybe," Mrs. Bee said. "Maybe not. Couldn't you go and shoo her back inside or something? It might be, if she saw you coming, she'd just get up and go in by herself, anyway—and you wouldn't have to do anything. It's worth a try, don't you think?''

No, he didn't think, but he didn't say so. His legs hurt. He was tired. And pineapple-coconut-cream-cake hungry. He looked out the window. It was raining as hard as ever, and Meehan was still sitting there. He drew a quiet breath and glanced at Mrs. Bee. Her whole frail little body was saying one thing and one thing only—*Please!*

Ah, damn it.

"Okay," he said. "I'll go shoo her. She's not going to like it—I'm going to catch hell for it. But I'll go.''

"I'll get the umbrella," Mrs. Bee said, scurrying away.

He peered through the window again, hoping that Meehan would be gone. She wasn't.

Mrs. Bee came back with a big multicolored golf umbrella. He took it and hobbled toward the back door.

"You're a good boy, Calvin," she said as he stepped out into the rain.

Doyle opened the umbrella. He could feel Mrs. Bee's eyes on him all the way across the backyard. Which was just as well, because he probably wouldn't have gone otherwise.

It was hard walking on the rough, wet ground, but he didn't have a choice if he wanted to get this over with. Which he did. It would take him too long to hobble down Mrs. Bee's driveway to the sidewalk and then around the hedge and back up Meehan's drive to where she was still sitting on the bench—the key word here being "still."

Oh, he had the "hunt the hill, get the hill" mind-set, all right.

And what the hell was wrong with Meehan that she would be sitting out in the rain like this?

He'd find out soon enough, he guessed, if he kept going. He could see her plainly through the hedge. She seemed to be completely lost in thought. He could have yelled at her at any point, but he didn't. He just kept slogging along, pulling the cane out of the mud with every step. She didn't even notice him until he was right on her and held the umbrella over her head. Nice touch, the umbrella, he thought. Gave the trip—ill-advised though it may be—a purpose.

Meehan looked up at him. She didn't say anything; neither did he. And she wasn't bawling. That was a plus.

With some effort, he continued to stand and hold the umbrella over them both—a futile gesture at this point in her case. She was wet to the skin.

She frowned. Just enough of one to let him know he was on dangerous ground here. Not exactly news.

Hunt the hill, get the hill.

"So," he said pleasantly. "What's new?"

She gave a sharp sigh. "Bugs, what are you doing here?"

"Holding the umbrella," he said reasonably.

"What do you want?"

"What do I *want?* Well, let's see. I want a cold beer, for one thing. And I want somebody to drive me to some loud, smoky, possibly sleazy place where I can get one. Maybe a big thick steak with a pile of fried onions, too, while I'm at it. Since that's not going to happen, I guess I want to stand right here—until I can shoo you back into the house."

"I don't want to be 'shooed,'" she assured him. "And you can mind your own damn business."

"Oh, I know that. I tried to mind it, believe me. It didn't work, though. See, you're not exactly what I would call behaving here—or does the 'behave and don't upset Mrs. Bee' thing just go for me?"

"What are you talking about!"

"Mrs. Bee! She's all worried about you sitting out here in the rain like this."

"She doesn't have to worry."

"Yeah, well, maybe so. But you know how she is. And I hate to say it, but I was getting a little uneasy about you myself. This is not like you."

"What did you and Mrs. Bee do, watch everything out the window?"

"Pretty much," he said. Personally, he'd always found it a lot easier to just tell the truth in most situations—unless it involved some gung-ho officer. It was too much trouble keeping stories straight. He suspected that Meehan was the same way, especially when she was working. He had always believed whatever she said, anyway. The whole time he was in the hospital, whenever he needed to know what was what with the pain in his legs or the burns on his hands or why he was running yet another fever, she was the one he always wanted to ask, because he knew she'd tell him straight.

He kept looking at her. She was upset, all right, and once again he was glad she wasn't bawling. He didn't know what to do when women cried—strong women, that is. Women like Rita. Or Specialist 4 Santos. Santos was a damned good soldier, but she always bawled when she had to make a jump. He didn't know why, and he wasn't sure she did, either. She would cry like she wasn't crying, and nobody knew what was up with that. The jumpmasters certainly weren't crazy about it. But, she always lined up like everybody else and hopped right out the door when she was supposed to. It was just…damned unsettling.

Tears weren't a big deal with most women. But Rita and Santos—and Meehan, if she happened to break down—were an altogether different situation.

He kept checking Meehan out, just in case. She caught him at it, and she started to say something but didn't. She looked away, down the driveway in the direction lover boy had gone.

He waited.

And waited.

The rain beat down on the umbrella. A car went down the street, its heavy bass speakers pounding.

Somebody somewhere threw something heavy into a metal trash can.

"So did you get dumped or what?" he asked finally—and that got her attention.

She stared at him a long time before she answered. "Yes," she said finally.

"Yeah, well, it's been that kind of a day," he said with the assurance of a man who'd been there.

He maneuvered the cane so that he could press one hand into his thigh. Both legs were beginning to hurt like hell. He tried to shift his weight a little. It didn't help a bit. When he looked up again, Meehan wasn't frowning anymore. It occurred to him that she was a lot nicer looking when she didn't frown.

"Did you go to the wedding?" she asked.

"I went," he admitted.

"Everybody was all dressed up, I guess."

"Oh, yeah."

"Even you?"

"Especially me. I looked so good it's a wonder the ceremony even took place."

She gave a slight smile. It faded almost immediately.

"So how was it?" she asked a little too gently for him to maintain his bravado.

"It was—" he stopped and took a breath "—it was hell. Mostly."

"Poor old Bugs," she said.

He grinned. "At least I ain't sitting out in the rain over it."

To his surprise she laughed. She had a nice laugh. Definitely she should laugh a lot more than she did.

"I allow myself to do one really stupid thing at least once a year," she said after a moment.

"And this is it, huh?"

"This is it. I wish I could think of some really cool way to get out of it." She was still smiling a little, and she made an attempt to stand up. He tried to move out of her way. The pain in his legs intensified, and he couldn't keep from bending forward.

"What's the matter?" she asked, dodging the umbrella before he clunked her in the head with it.

"Hurts," was all he could manage.

"Well, no wonder. Coming out in the rain like this."

"Yeah, and who's fault...would that be? If you don't mind me...pointing that...out."

"Okay, okay. Do you want me to help you?" she asked, he guessed because she'd been around enough banged-up soldiers to know that assistance wasn't always welcome.

"No."

"How long has it been since you took something for pain?"

"About three...weeks..." he said through gritted teeth.

"You're not taking the prescription the doctor ordered for you?"

"Can't stay awake. You know…me. Don't want to…miss anything."

"How long has it been since you've eaten?"

"I'm hurting…not…hungry," he said. Which wasn't precisely the truth. Not a lie exactly, more a matter of priorities. He'd planned on eating. He'd been about to zero in on Mrs. Bee's cake with the pineapple-and-coconut-cream icing—but he got sucked into coming over here. And that fact just added to his current aggravation.

"You're exhausted, is what you are. You've done too much today, and you've probably been feeling too sorry for yourself to eat—"

"I ate, I ate!"

He tried to take a step or two and was pitiful at it.

"Okay," she said. "That's enough. You're getting the shakes. Just stand here a second and then we'll hobble that way." She pointed toward her back door.

"No…thanks," he managed to say.

"You should have taken a pain pill—especially today."

"I don't take them, Meehan, unless I have to. Just special occasions. When it hurts…really bad."

"Well, what do you call this?"

"A minor setback…brought on by people not…behaving."

"Very funny. Now go that way."

"I'll be okay in a…minute."

"I *said* go. It's closer than trying to get back to Mrs. Bee's. You're going to fall on your face. You've let the muscles in your legs go into spasm—"

"Right," he said. "I...*let* them. Just for the...hell of it."

"Oh, quit whining and let's go. You can get off your feet for a little while and then you can run along home and give Mrs. Bee your report."

She wouldn't take no for an answer. He hobbled in the direction she was pushing him—but he didn't like it.

"Take the...umbrella," he said at one point.

She took it, but his not carrying the umbrella didn't help him walk much better. She had to hold it way up in the air to keep him covered.

"Try putting your hand on my shoulder," she said.

"It won't...help."

"Do it."

He did as she ordered, bearing down hard with his next step. "This is all your—"

"Fault," she finished with him. "I got that part."

"So how come he...dumped you?" Doyle asked bluntly. The question was entirely inappropriate, but pain apparently made him reckless. Besides that, he actually wanted to know, and this seemed like as good a time as any to ask.

"It's none of your damned business," she said for the second time.

"Right. But since I've gone to all this trouble, I ought to at least be able to...give Mrs. Bee the details. We live for drama and pathos."

"You and Mrs. Bee need to get out more."

"Ain't that the truth," he said, glancing at her. He'd made her smile again. Maybe the bust-up with the boyfriend wasn't as serious as it looked out the window.

Still, she'd been sitting out in the rain all that time.

"Maybe you can work it out," he said.

"Work what out?"

"The thing with the boyfriend."

"Don't think so," she said, catching the back of his shirt when he began to list.

They finally reached the patio. She managed to open her back door and hold it with one foot while she closed the umbrella. He shuffled dutifully inside. The house obviously had central air, because the room was cool and quiet. There was a television, an easy chair, a whole row of plants under a big window, and a couch with a startled white cat on it. He didn't like cats, or so he assumed. He'd never been around any, except the wild "barn" cats that used to live on his grandfather's farm when he was a little boy. That relationship had been very one-sided. Every day, he'd toss them the table scraps his grandmother allotted them, and every day they hissed and spat and ran like hell.

The cat jumped down from the couch and disappeared.

"Sit down," Meehan said unnecessarily. He couldn't have made it any farther if he'd wanted to. He plopped down heavily on the couch where the cat had been.

The pain was less now that he was off his feet, but not much. He leaned back and closed his eyes. When he opened them again, Meehan had gone someplace, and the cat was sitting on the couch arm.

"Take a hike," he said to it.

It continued to sit there, giving him its rapt attention. It was kind of unnerving. He'd never had an animal stare at him like that—or at least not one that was up to any good.

Meehan came back with a towel around her neck and one of those small electric blankets for couch potatoes in her hands. He sat there awkwardly, because he wasn't sure what she planned to do with it and because he was in her house more or less against his will.

"I didn't know you had a cat," he said in an inane attempt at making conversation. She bent down, plugged the blanket into a nearby outlet. She was wearing shorts, and he appreciated it.

The cat gave an inquisitive, rolling chirp and looked at Meehan expectantly.

"No, he doesn't," Meehan said to the cat. "But he would, if he had to."

She was smiling slightly. He got it right off the

bat. She was giving him the business here, and enjoying it. The big tough soldier wasn't sure what to do about the cat, much less her talking to it.

But she had no idea she was dealing with Doyle, the Supercool. Two could play this game.

"Doesn't what?" he asked to put her on the spot.

She dropped the blanket over his bare legs.

"Barbecue cats," she said without missing a beat. "She's the only survivor of a coyote attack on her and her litter mates. She's very concerned about whether or not she's in someone's food chain."

"Don't blame her. Where did she run into a coyote?"

"A friend's place in the mountains. She was just a kitten, and she took up residence in my shirt pocket while I was there—so I brought her home. She doesn't get out much, either. Of course, in her case, it's by choice—I couldn't get her out the door with a crowbar. I don't know about you and Mrs. Bee."

"Well, it's not by choice with me," he said. But the real truth was that the two guys he had called friends had been killed in the same helicopter crash. He missed the sorry sons-of-bitches more than he cared to admit, and thus far he hadn't gone looking for replacements.

Meehan was busy drying her hair with the towel.

"So tell me," she said out from under it. "Why do they call you 'Bugs'?"

He glanced at the cat. "I went outside my food chain," he said. "The survival-training thing."

"You weren't the only one to do that, were you?"

"I was the only one to throw up," he said, and she laughed again. Easily. Pleasantly. He hadn't been trying to be cute. He'd been telling the truth again—but he was beginning to feel pretty damned witty here.

He stretched his legs out in front of him. He wouldn't have thought the blanket would help, especially in July, but the pain was already beginning to lessen. "I'm going to have to get me one of these," he said.

"You can have that one," she said.

"No, I didn't mean—"

"I know you didn't. I have another. Actually, I have two others. My sisters seem to think I have no other way to keep warm. Take it."

He looked at her. She meant it.

"Well, okay. Thanks."

"You're welcome."

She disappeared again, and when she came back she had an apple in her hand. "Eat that," she said, throwing it to him. "Put your feet up."

She left him sitting there—with the cat. After a moment he maneuvered both legs onto a nearby ottoman. Then, he occupied himself eating the apple and looking around the room. Nice place. Neat. Clean. He could see several framed photographs on a table—little kids mostly. Or maybe the same two kids—a boy and a girl—at different ages.

Hers?

He didn't think so. At least, he'd never heard anyone mention that she had kids.

The cat finally made her move, stepping carefully onto the blanket on his lap and then standing a moment before cautiously lying down. He sat there stiffly, trying to decide how badly he minded. The cat wasn't hurting anything, he supposed, not even his bare legs under the blanket. After a moment he tentatively let his hand rest on its fur. It began to purr immediately. He couldn't hear it, though. He could feel it with his fingertips.

"Just as long as nobody sees me," he told the little beast before it got too comfortable.

He took a quiet breath. He was so tired. After a while, the cat stretched out across his knees. The added warmth was not...unpleasant.

He closed his eyes. He heard a telephone ringing somewhere and Meehan answer it. The conversation was brief, and, as far as he could tell, nonhostile.

Must not be the boyfriend.

He heard the rain, and a strong gust of wind against the house. And then he heard nothing.

Chapter Two

Something's wrong with my hand.

The realization penetrated his sleep and wouldn't leave. His hand was tingling. No...not tingling. Vibrating.

He opened his eyes.

The cat.

It was purring. It had moved off his legs and was sharing half—more than half—of the heated throw. His hand rested heavily on its back.

"What time is it?" Doyle said out loud, in spite of the fact that he didn't hear Meehan anywhere.

The cat rolled into a ball and hid its face in its paws. He looked around the room. It was still daylight.

Wrong, he thought immediately. It wasn't "still" anything. The sun was shining, and it was on the morning side of the house. He attempted to move his legs off the ottoman—and regretted it immediately. He rarely slept the whole night through, but apparently he'd done just that, and he was paying dearly for the inactivity.

His cane was propped against the couch. It had a note taped to the handle, one direct and to the point: "Latrine—doorway straight ahead. Kitchen—doorway to left. Coffeepot comes on at five-thirty."

He could smell coffee, come to think of it, but first things first. With considerable effort he managed to get to his feet and then make it to the latrine and back, closely supervised by a meowing cat all the way. It ran along in front of him into the kitchen and pointedly sat down facing a base cabinet door.

"What?" Doyle said in response to yet another of its inquisitive chirps and in spite of his determination not to talk to it. The cat immediately stood, did a kind of four-pawed, feline ballet pivot and sat down again. And stared at him.

"Can't help you," he said. "Just passing through."

And he intended to do just that, but the coffeemaker gurgled. He looked in that direction. There was another note taped to it. He hobbled over to read it:

"Cups in cabinet in front of you. Unplug pot when you leave."

The coffee smelled great, and he was never one to pass up an invitation. He reached up and opened the cabinet door and took out a shiny black coffee mug. He poured some coffee into it while the cat did figure eights at his feet.

"Nine point six," he said, looking down. "Maybe seven."

The cat ran to the base cabinet door again and meowed loudly.

"Okay, okay. I get it. That's the chow door and the MRE's are in there, right?"

He hobbled over and opened the door. A small box full of pouches of cat food sat on the bottom shelf—the feline version of Meals Ready to Eat. With some difficulty, he got one of them out.

"See?" he said to the cat. "I'm not as dumb as I look." He might not speak the language, but he'd had plenty of practice muddling through, anyway, in his time. In the Balkans. In Haiti. In Korea.

He shook off the feeling of loss the memory of a healthier and more useful time gave him and glanced around for something to commandeer for a cat food dish. He saw nothing particularly appropriate, so he tore the pouch open and down one side and placed—dropped—it on a paper towel on the floor. The cat didn't mind roughing it in the least.

He walked painfully back to his coffee. It was really good, and he took the cup to the table and eventually maneuvered himself into a chair. He stretched both arms over his head and yawned noisily, wondering idly where his hostess had gotten to. Maybe the boyfriend had had second thoughts about the situation. Maybe he'd regrouped and come back here last night with his hat in his hand—or his bag of bagels—and Meehan, overwhelmed by his generosity and not wanting to explain what the gimp was doing snoozing on her couch, had trotted off with him to his place.

Doyle picked up the coffee cup and immediately put it down again. He didn't much care for that scenario. It didn't fit his idea of what Kate Meehan was like, for one thing. She wasn't the kind of woman who would let a man jerk her around, especially one who had done his dead level best to make her cry. She was the kind who would—

He gave a sharp exhalation of breath and repositioned his aching legs. What the hell did he know about Meehan and her situation?

Nothing.

Still, he was kind of surprised that she would go off and just leave him alone in her house. On the other hand, she'd trusted him enough to inflict him on Mrs. Bee. It looked as if she trusted him enough to leave him all alone with the Meehan family silver, too.

The doorbell abruptly rang—way too early for callers in Doyle's opinion. He toyed with the idea of ignoring it, then decided that it might be Meehan with her arms full, and the least he could do was let her into her own house.

He struggled to his feet and then to the door—the wrong door. The doorbell rang again, and he hobbled in the opposite direction, this time with a cat escort.

The boyfriend stood on the patio with his little white bag and a cardboard coffee cup holder holding *two* cups.

"This ought to be good," Doyle said to the cat. He opened the door wide and stood waiting, enjoying the man's startled look much more than he should have. But—as he'd told Meehan—he didn't get out much. He had to find his entertainments where and when he could.

"I'm…looking for Katherine," the boyfriend said warily.

"Katie's not here," Doyle said, using Mrs. Bee's version of Meehan's given name for no other purpose than to annoy the man who had taken off and left her standing in the rain.

If at all possible.

The man frowned.

Definitely possible, Doyle decided.

"Where is she?" the boyfriend asked pointedly. He was not happy about this situation *at all*. Meehan was supposed to be exactly where he'd left her, no doubt. And she certainly wasn't supposed to be entertaining another man.

"Don't know," Doyle said.

"When will she be back?"

"Don't know," Doyle said, continuing his effort to be helpful.

"What are *you* doing in her house?" the man asked next, his Mr. Rich *and* Cool image getting away from him.

"Not much. Sleeping. Drinking coffee. Feeding the cat. You want me to take that?" Doyle asked of the little white bag and the plastic cups in the cardboard holder.

"No, I don't," the man snapped. He stalked away and dumped the white bag and the coffee in the roll-out trash can as he passed it.

"Want me to tell her you came by?" Doyle called. And made a fool of yourself?

The boyfriend didn't answer. He hopped into his very nice silver car and backed noisily out the drive.

The cat chirped at Doyle's feet. "Why didn't you stop me?" he asked it. "Now he's really vexed."

The cat made a different kind of noise and executed another one of its four-pawed dance turns.

"Nice dresser, though," Doyle said. He closed the door and hobbled back into the kitchen.

He finished the rest of his coffee standing up and put the empty cup on the top rack of the dishwasher. It was a lot harder to get the make-do cat food dish off the floor than to put it down there, but he eventually managed. There was nothing to do now but attempt the long walk across the yard to Mrs. Bee's. He was halfway to the back door when he remembered that he was supposed to unplug the coffee-maker.

As was its custom, the cat accompanied him in both directions, and when he opened the back door again, it sniffed the air but made no attempt to go outside.

"Stay alert," he said as he hobbled through. "Coyotes are sneaky bastards."

Doyle pulled the door closed after him and paused for a moment on the patio. The morning was cool, washed clean by yesterday's rain. Meehan's array of wind chimes tinkled softly in the breeze—glass, melodic chrome tubes and tiny brass bells, and, every now and then, a dull and hollow clunk of bamboo. Flowers grew in numerous pots and hanging baskets, most of which he couldn't identify. He recognized the red and purple petunias, but he had no idea whatsoever about the green thing that smelled like lemons. His knowledge of plants was limited to farm crops and survival-training edibles. His knowledge of Kate Meehan was limited, as well. Who would have thought she liked these kinds of things?

An assortment of birds flew back and forth to the fancy blue-and-gray ceramic bird feeder, all of them vying for a perch. He stood and watched the no-guts-no-glory chickadees out maneuver the larger birds for more than their fair share of the sunflower seeds. What they lacked in size they made up for in speed and audacity. There was a lot to be said for both qualities, and he longed for the time when he might regain at least one of them.

Look and learn, he thought, his mind immediately going to his grandfather. The old man used to say that all the time.

Look and learn.

Listen and learn.

Live and learn.

Pop Doyle had believed that life's lessons were everywhere if a man had enough sense to stop and pay attention—which had amused his grandson in a way that only a smartass punk kid could be amused. Doyle knew the truth of it now, though. Now when the old man was long gone, and he couldn't tell him so.

Doyle had stood in one place too long, and he maneuvered himself slowly down the brick patio steps. He definitely could have used Meehan's shoulder to hold on to.

In spite of the pain, he opted for the long way around the hedge and headed down Meehan's drive-way to the street. It was slow going, his progress accomplished in fits and starts and nothing like the days when he went running at six-thirty in the morning no matter what.

He missed it, damn it! He once had a sense of accomplishment, and he had taken such pride in being one of the best. It was so hard to give it all up.

No. It was so hard to have it all taken away.

A passing car honked, and he caught a glimpse

of a rolled-up, OD camouflage sleeve waving out the open window as it disappeared around the corner. Somebody who knew him, Doyle guessed. Or knew *of* him. Somebody who still had legs that worked like they were supposed to and who was lucky enough to have somewhere to go and something to do.

He took a deep breath and fought down the self-pity that threatened to overwhelm him. One foot in front of the other, that's all it took. Pop Doyle and his drill sergeant said so.

Doyle had worked up a sweat by the time he reached Mrs. Bee's back door. He expected it to be locked, but it wasn't. Mrs. Bee was awake and busily ironing pillowcases in the still-cool, wide central hallway. He expected the third degree, too, but she only smiled and kept ironing.

"You're a good boy, Calvin," she said when he was halfway up the stairs.

"Yes, ma'am," he said dutifully. "That would be me."

Mrs. Bee still didn't ask him anything about his mission of mercy, so he kept going. Not that he had much to report. Meehan had been dumped—which Mrs. Bee likely already realized if she'd witnessed even half as much of the scene next door as he had. He'd have to hand it to his landlady, though. She said she only wanted Meehan in out of the rain, and that accomplished, she apparently didn't need to know whatever sordid details he might have uncovered *or* why he was just now reporting in.

He made it to his quarters eventually. Unlike the downstairs hall, the apartment was hot and stuffy. He switched the air conditioner to high and stood in front of the cold blast of air, staring at nothing. The morning stretched endlessly before him, as did the afternoon, the week, the rest of his life.

He fried some bacon, then didn't eat it. He maneuvered painfully to the floor instead and did an altogether impressive number of stretches and "ab crunches" just to keep the physical therapist happy. Then he showered and dressed in the uniform of the day—PT-gray running shorts and T-shirt—and running shoes that were hell to get tied.

As a reward he picked up his guitar and managed to strum what might pass for an actual melody. Then he refined it. Embellished it. Sang along.

And didn't let his mind go anywhere near Rita Warren.

He was getting better at playing the guitar, helicopter crash or no helicopter crash. He had never had much of a singing voice, but he didn't let that stop him. If he felt like singing, he sang. The residual huskiness from the fire and who knew how many hospital breathing tubes didn't particularly concern him. The good news was that his fingers were much more inclined to do what he wanted them to do of late. They still hurt, of course, but what else was new?

Just to break the monotony, he hobbled to the window a couple of times to look out at Meehan's house. Absolutely nothing was going on there. She hadn't come home yet, and the boyfriend hadn't returned with another little white bagel bag.

It took considerable willpower on his part not to make a third trip to the window.

"I have *got* to get out of here," he said to no one in particular. He was becoming way too interested in the neighbors—sort of like the guy with the broken leg in the Hitchcock movie he'd stayed up late watching the other night. Of course, that guy had had all kinds of people to spy on. Doyle only had Meehan and the boyfriend—and it suddenly occurred to him that he wasn't all that interested in the boyfriend. He was interested in Meehan, and he was letting himself get all concerned about her just like he did with Rita. He needed to go somewhere, do *something,* anything to take his mind off his troubles—and hers.

He looked at the noisy, battery-operated clock on the wall and sighed.

Oh-nine-thirty.

He could call Sergeant Beltran. Beltran would have transportation here in a heartbeat. Doyle could go to the grocery store—except that he didn't need groceries. Or to the barber shop—except that he didn't need a haircut, either. And he had way too much pride to let it be known that he just needed company—somebody to baby-sit.

He ate the bacon after all and read yesterday's newspaper. His dress uniform hung on a hanger on the half-open closet door, and he hobbled over to put it away. He smiled slightly to himself as he hung it in the closet. He hadn't exaggerated too much when he'd told Meehan he had looked good at Rita's wedding. At least he'd regained enough weight so that he wore the uniform instead of the other way around. Except for the fact that he couldn't half walk, he was a lean, mean fighting machine.

Hoo-ah!

"There it is," he said out loud. His audacity. It was back after all. And as long as he was up and moving, he got a can of cola out of the refrigerator and hunted up an empty plastic grocery bag. Then he took himself out into the summer heat of the upstairs hallway, hesitating for a moment to secure the can in the bag before he tackled the back stairs. He had no real plan other than to get himself and the can down the numerous steps in one piece. Once he accomplished that, then he'd decide what to do. No problem there. Given his physical limitations, the list of possibilities was very short.

He ultimately ended up sprawled on the cushions on the wicker swing on the shady front porch. It was hot, though—shade or no shade—but he could put up with the heat for the prospect of a little entertainment. Something was bound to happen—mail delivery, garbage pick up, a dog fight.

Something.

Anything.

"There you are," someone said behind him, making him jump. He turned in the swing to see Meehan standing with the throw she'd said he could have over her arm. She must have come down the back stairs after he had. She was wearing her nurse clothes and she looked sleep deprived and tired.

"For a man who can't get around you're hard to track down," she said. "You forgot this." She draped the throw over the back of the swing.

"No—hey—I don't want to put you out."

"I told you I have three. I can spare one. Use it when you get the muscle spasms in your legs. If you're not going to take your pain med, it'll help as much as anything."

"You really don't have to—"

"I know that, Doyle. Just take it, okay? I've had a very rough night. Don't make me hurt you."

He couldn't keep from smiling, because it was nice of her to go to all this trouble and because she was being—and looking—more than a little cute here, in spite of the obviously rough night.

Cute.

She'd twisted her hair up and fastened it with some kind of clasp thing—but some strands had come loose and fell around her face, making her look kind of soft and rumpled and just out of bed. He tried not to stare at her. There was absolutely no doubt about it—and Meehan cute was even more jarring than Meehan with wind chimes and lemon-scented flowers. He wondered idly why he hadn't noticed it before. No, he must have noticed. He paid attention to things like that—half-dead or not.

"Okay, okay," he said. "But there's one condition."

"What kind of condition?"

"You let me buy you a steak in appreciation. A really big one—with fried onions and a cold beer. Today. Anywhere you say."

She was watching him closely, and he tried not to look as needy as he felt.

"Today," she said after a long moment.

"Right."

"In appreciation for the throw."

"Right."

"Are you that desperate to get out?"

"Yeah," he said truthfully, and she laughed.

"I'm desperate," he said. "And I want to say thanks. You helped me out yesterday."

"I think maybe the help was mutual."

"Yeah, but I had Mrs. Bee's foot in my back. You didn't. Maybe we could just kill two birds with one dinner and call it even. Simple as that."

She was still watching him, and he let himself look into her eyes. Interesting eyes. Hazel blue. Nice.

"Don't you—?" she started to ask, then abruptly broke off. He had no problem guessing the direction she'd been about to take. She wanted to know why he was bothering her when he could be going out with his buddies—until she suddenly remembered that he didn't have any buddies…and why.

"So?" he persisted. At this point he'd take whatever he could get—even a pity outing.

"Thanks, but I can't. I just got off work and I still have some things to do. I have to sleep at some point. Besides, it's really not necessary for you—"

"Okay," he interrupted. "Just a thought."

She began to walk away from him toward the porch steps, but she stopped before she got there and looked back. She didn't say anything, and neither did he. He could almost feel her trying to make up her mind.

He waited. She definitely had questions, but for some reason she wasn't quite comfortable asking them.

"It would have to be late," she said finally.

"No problem—fine with me. Did I say you get to drive?"

"I guessed as much."

"Around nineteen hundred then? Or whenever. I'll be here."

She was still looking at him, still sitting on the fence about it. "Okay. I'll see you when I wake up. I get to pick the place, right?"

"Right," he said.

She was smiling again—this smile a kind of spider-to-the-fly one that challenged him—and made him a little leery about her expectations. And he'd seen the boyfriend up close. There was money there and a lot of it. He, on the other hand...

"Maybe you should bring along some plastic," he said. "Just in case."

"Plastic," she said as if she wasn't sure she'd heard right.

"Correct. Hey, you always got to have a contingency plan, Meehan."

"Right. And you military guys are all alike," she said, the smile broadening. "See you later, Specialist."

She turned and ran lightly down the steps.

"Outstanding," he said under his breath—and he didn't mean just her capitulation. He watched her as long as he could, infinitely pleased with himself, because he thought she was as surprised that she'd accepted his offer as he was. In any event he was actually going to get that steak and beer, and the company wasn't half-bad, either. Meehan was used to men who had to hobble, and she knew all about Rita. He wouldn't have to put up a macho front if he didn't want to. He could just kick back and be his miserable self.

He took a deep breath, fully aware of how little he had been thinking of Rita just now. And there was the other thing. He had just had a stellar opportunity to tell Meehan that the boyfriend had made a reconnaissance bright and early this morning— and, for whatever reason, he hadn't taken it.

Chapter Three

She is going to bail.

It didn't take a genius to figure that out. She was late by anyone's calculation, even with parameters as loosely defined as these had been. And she didn't look as if she was planning anything so ordinary as a steak and a beer with a broken-down army specialist. And, on top of that, she'd caught him waiting on the front porch swing like the last puppy at the pound.

The boyfriend's back, Doyle suddenly thought as she stepped up on the porch. And the mission had been scrubbed. He sat looking at her, wondering what to say.

Nothing, he decided. She was the one bailing.

He'd let her do the talking. She could talk, and he would just look.

Man, she cleaned up good. In all his years in the army, he'd never gotten used to the way some women could pull that off—looking one way all the time until you more or less forgot they were even female—and then doing whatever it was they did to end up looking like *this*.

Meehan was wearing a dress. He'd never seen her in a dress. It was colorful—really flowery. It made him think of watercolors—and it was kind of floaty and thin.

Thin.

He couldn't see through it—but he kept expecting to. It wasn't an all-tarted-up kind of dress or anything like that. It was just…attention getting. Her shoulders were bare, except for little string straps, and soft looking, even in this light. Smooth. Touchable. He could easily imagine how good they would feel if he ran his hands over them, how good they would smell…

Don't go there! he thought, but it didn't keep him from wondering.

Like what? Flowers? Roses—or something citrus maybe. But nice.

One of the little string straps dropped off her shoulder.

Very nice…

Take it easy, Doyle!

This was Meehan here—and he was acting like she was a real woman or something.

"Bugs, are you listening to me?" she said.

"Sure. It's too late to go out."

"You think so."

He frowned. "I thought that was what you said."

"It was a question, Doyle. *Is* it too late to go out?"

"With me, you mean."

She tried to look into his eyes. "You took a pain pill, didn't you?"

"No," he said, grinning. "But I think we need to start over here. *You* asked *me* if it's too late to go."

"Right. Is it?"

"No way. I'm starving."

"Can you wait a half hour or so?"

He didn't think he could wait five minutes, so he didn't answer her, for no other reason than the way she looked. That alone was worth the delay.

"I didn't mean to be this late—but I just woke up. I got hung up with a family thing after I left here, and I still need to make a phone call or two."

"A family thing," he repeated, because he'd been expecting her to say she was sorry, but she had to run along now, with the bagel guy.

"Right. I've got three sisters—two older, one younger. Unfortunately, they think up things for me to do for entertainment."

"I hear that," he said. "I've got one of those myself. So what are you fixing?"

"My uncle Patrick."

"And your job would be...?"

"He's a widower. He's not taking care of himself. I get to call him up and yell at him."

"Poor Uncle Patrick," he said, trying not to grin.

"What is that supposed to mean?"

"It means I've been there."

"I've never yelled at you," she said, clearly believing it.

"Sure you have."

"I have not."

"Oh, then that must have been somebody in leg casts who just *looked* like me."

A smile was just about to get away from her. "Why did I yell at you?"

"No reason whatsoever. I was totally innocent. I guarantee it."

"That'll be the day—so are we on for tonight or not?"

"On," he said. "Definitely on." Things were getting better and better here.

"Then I'll be back," she said.

He expected her to go home, but she went inside Mrs. Bee's house instead. She didn't stay long. If she'd used Mrs. Bee's phone to yell at Uncle Patrick, she'd made it short and sweet.

"That was fast," he said as she stepped out onto the porch again.

"I delegated the situation to Mrs. Bee—well, actually she volunteered. She knows Uncle Patrick, and she's a lot more tactful than I am. So let's go. She wants us to take Thelma and Louise," Meehan added as he heaved himself up off the swing.

"The more, the merrier," he said, because he still couldn't believe that she had actually shown up. At this point he didn't care who went along, and he was only mildly concerned about the possibility that he might have to swing feeding two more people.

"What?" he said, because of the look Meehan was giving him.

"Well, I expected you to be a little happier about it."

"About what?"

"Thelma and Louise. Will you pay attention?"

"I'm happy. I don't think I know who they are, though—or maybe I do. Church ladies, right?"

"No," Meehan said, laughing. "Thelma and Louise is a *car*." She held up a set of keys and dangled them.

"Okay," he said, still not getting it.

"A 1966 Thunderbird convertible."

"You are kidding me. Like the one in the movie, you mean?"

"Except this one is red. Leather seats. Mint condition."

"You are *kidding* me," he said again.

"Nope. The late Mr. Bee gave it to her, brand-new, for her fiftieth birthday. She's called it Thelma and Louise ever since she saw the movie. He didn't want her to be depressed about hitting the half-century mark.''

''Did it work?''

''Well, driving it certainly cheers *me* up. She wants me to blow it out on the interstate.''

''You know how to do that, I guess,'' he said, trying not to smile.

''You just hold on to your hat, soldier.''

She led the way down the steps, and she didn't offer to help him. He liked that about her—that she didn't act as if she even noticed that he was incapacitated. Unless he was about to fall on his face.

Everything was working pretty well at the moment, though. Some pain. Not too bad. He wished he'd dressed up a little. He'd traded the PT outfit for civilian cargo shorts and a blue golf shirt, but no way was he in any kind of league with that dress.

The car was carefully locked away in a wooden building in the backyard, one Doyle had seen a million times and never wondered about.

He followed Meehan in that direction, then abruptly stopped.

''What's the matter?'' she asked, looking back at him.

''Before we get too far along here, I better tell you the boyfriend came by this morning—in case you want to do something about it.''

''Oh, I know,'' she said.

''You know? What did he do? Call to report someone had broken into your house?''

"Something like that," she said.

He started walking again. "And you said?"

"Nothing."

"Nothing?"

"I don't have to explain what you were doing in my house to anyone—except maybe my sisters. Those three would definitely have to have an explanation."

He grinned and continued walking to the edge of the driveway, waiting well out of the way while Meehan unlocked the padlock on the door of the outbuilding.

"Damn," he said under his breath as she eased the shiny red car out of the shed and into what was left of daylight. The vehicle was nothing short of spectacular. How had he missed knowing about this? The car was so fine it would be a privilege just to wash it. Mrs. Bee was full of surprises.

"How do you like it?" Meehan said through the open window.

"Damn," he said again.

"Exactly," Meehan said.

"So will the top go down?"

"No problem."

"Outstanding!" he said with every bit of the enthusiasm he felt.

He hobbled around to the other side. She had the top moving before he reached the passenger-side door. It took some doing for him to get himself inside, but he managed. He sat there for a moment, admiring everything—the seats, the dash—Meehan's legs. The radio worked, but it wasn't original. Mrs. Bee apparently liked her sounds. This one had FM bass-expander stereo.

He was beginning to feel like a kid on Christmas morning. Or the cowboy in the *Thelma and Louise* movie.

"So where are we going?" he asked when he'd finished appreciating everything.

"I'll leave that to you."

"No—you pick. Anywhere you want."

She looked at him for a moment in a way he couldn't quite figure out. Like she wasn't sure he meant it—and if he did, *why.*

But he did mean it. He didn't care where they went—of course, his ensemble limited the options.

She picked a place near the mall—the same one he would have picked actually.

"Parking lot is pretty crowded," she said as she pulled the car into a space.

"No, this is fine. They have great food."

"And beer," she said helpfully.

"And beer," he agreed.

"You might see someone you know here."

"You, too," he countered.

"I don't care."

"Well, me, neither," he assured her.

"This might work out then," she said.

"Damn straight."

"Can you walk that far? I can pull up to the door and let you out."

"No, I can make it." He opened the car door. He didn't want to be let out. He wanted to hobble across the parking lot in plain view—with her—so all those people neither one of them cared about could see them together and eat their sorry hearts out.

It was hard work, though. He had to stop once to rest before he could make it all the way to the door. There was a line, but the bench full of paratroopers in the crowded waiting area immediately cleared a place for him to sit down. His legs hurt badly enough for him to forego the macho stuff and take it. They even made room for Meehan—which was clearly not a hardship. He didn't miss the fact that they all appreciated her nonseethrough little dress as much as he did.

The place was rowdy this evening. A group in a far corner had started a swaying, hand-clapping sing-along with the song playing on the jukebox, he thought more because the refrain was the same as their basic training anthem than anything else.

"I like it! I love it! I want some more of it!"

Doyle couldn't keep from humming with them under his breath. He could smell the steaks grilling and the French fries and onions frying. He was in pure heaven.

It doesn't get much better than this, he thought.

He glanced at Meehan. She was smiling.

"What?" he asked.

"It's nice to see you enjoying yourself," she said.

He didn't reply. Meehan would know that, he supposed, if anybody would. She'd certainly seen him enough times when he wasn't enjoying himself, when he had a raging fever and was so out of it he hardly knew where he was. He *was* enjoying himself. *This* was a whole lot better than anything he'd participated in in months.

The seating hostess called a name.

"Hey, buddy, you take it," a soldier close to him said.

"Nah, that's all right."

"Go ahead! You can owe me."

Doyle looked at Meehan. She was waiting for him to decide if he wanted to accept the favor.

He did, and he got shakily to his feet—without help.

"Thanks a lot," Doyle said to him. "I appreciate it."

"Nice to have friends in high places," Meehan said as they followed the hostess to the table.

"Except he's not a friend. I don't know him."

"Then it's nice the way you guys look after each other," Meehan said.

"It's all part of the code," he said.

It was a small table for two, but it wasn't half bad. Not too close to the music and not too far away. And nowhere near the kitchen. With a little effort they might even be able to talk to each other.

He decided to give it a try.

"So how are you doing?" he asked.

"Me?" she said in surprise. "I'm fine. Why?"

"Well, you had what I would call a trying day yesterday. Today, too, maybe."

"I'm all right."

"Is it all over with the boyfriend, then?" He had no business asking that, but it just sort of fell out of his mouth. He wanted to know. He'd wanted to know all day.

"It's over."

"Maybe not. He came by this morning."

"He came by because he wants me to do everything I can to keep him from feeling guilty."

"So did you?"

"I hope not," she said, and he smiled.

A waitress came with two beers in frosty mugs—ones they hadn't ordered.

"Best wishes from the paratrooping people at table number seven," she said, plunking them down. Doyle looked in the direction she indicated with her elbow. He raised his mug to the men and women sitting a few tables away, some of whom looked familiar, none of whom he knew by name.

"Don't tell me, let me guess. You don't know them, either."

"Nope."

"Must be the haircut," she said—which very well could be the case. It was nothing if not indicative of his chosen profession.

A different waitress came to take their orders.

When she'd gone, a girl walked by the table, a girl who looked a lot like Rita from the back. She even tossed her long blond hair as she passed, just the way Rita always did. He watched her until she disappeared into the crowd still waiting to be seated.

"Poor old Bugs," Meehan said when he looked back at her.

"It's worse for you than it is for me," he said.

"Why do you say that?"

"Because I saw it coming. You didn't."

"Well, you've got me there."

"Don't worry," he said, lifting his mug. "We're going to be all right."

She lifted her beer in return, but she didn't drink much of it. "Maybe so," she said, smiling. "This was a good idea, anyway. Tell me about the wedding—who was there?"

He ran down the guest list, described how cute little Olivia had looked, and what they had to eat at the reception.

"What's the guy's name?" he asked at the end of his debriefing.

"What guy?"

"The bagel guy," he said.

"Bugs, this is—"

"None of my business," he finished for her. "I know, but I can't help it. It's a hobby of mine. I like to know things. It keeps me off the streets."

"Maybe you should find yourself a new hobby."

"This *is* a new hobby. I used to jump out of airplanes. So what does the bagel guy do for a living?"

"Real estate."

"Real estate. There's money there, huh?"

"I really don't know. So how are you and Mrs. Bee getting along?" she asked in a bold move to change the subject.

"Good so far. She's a nice old lady. I never did tell you I appreciate you getting me in there. Thanks."

"She likes you a lot."

"Does she?"

"Yes. She's says you're like Michael Mont."

"Who's Michael Mont?"

"He was a character in a book. *The Forsyte Saga,* I think. John Galsworthy."

"I don't know anything about that," he said, but he didn't doubt that Mrs. Bee had said it. She used to be an English teacher; she would know about characters in books. "So what kind of guy would this Michael Mont be?"

"I don't know. Kind, probably. Optimistic."

He looked at her, wondering if that was what *she* thought—or what she thought Mrs. Bee thought. It didn't matter, really. They were both wrong. He wasn't either of those things.

"So what's the bagel guy's name," he asked again after a time.

"Why do you want to know?" Meehan said, clearly exasperated.

''Because I think I see him in line waiting to get in.''

She gave a quiet sigh, but she didn't turn around to look. Doyle wondered idly if she knew the guy would be coming here and that was the reason she'd picked this particular place.

No, he decided. Her whole demeanor had changed. If anything, she had on her ''lock and load'' face. She didn't know he'd be here.

Doyle was going to ask if she wanted to cut and run, but the steaks came, and the conversation switched to that. When it came to New York strips and onions, the cook in this place really knew how to shine. Meehan concentrated on her food, looking up from time to time to talk to him. Maybe she was having to work at it, but if she tried to locate the boyfriend's whereabouts, he didn't see her do it.

When they were nearly finished eating, he ordered two pieces of French apple pie to go. After the waitress had gone, he realized that Meehan was looking at him.

''What?''

''Nothing. I was just wondering where you were going to put all that pie.''

''One of them is for Mrs. Bee,'' he said. ''She came up with some outstanding transportation for this operation. She ought to get a little something out of it.''

''To Mrs. Bee,'' Meehan said, lifting her beer mug.

"And those like her!" he countered, lifting his own mug.

"And damn few of them left!" they said together, laughing.

Well, check this out, he thought suddenly. He was having a good time here—dumped and heartbroken or not. Everything was great. The food. The beer. The music.

Meehan.

Somebody had punched up a real "oldie goldie" on the jukebox. The sing-along table in the far corner had quieted down, but one nearby started up. A bunch of old guys, ex-paratroopers from the sound of them—Vietnam vets, maybe—and boy, were they ready to take up the slack.

One of them slid his chair back from the table— then kept sliding in their direction.

"Hey, Sweet Darlin'," he said to Meehan in keeping with the spirit of the song playing in the background, and Doyle braced himself to have to conk some pushy old guy over the head with his cane, brother soldier or not.

"Hey, Jake," she said. "How's it going?"

"I'm good as new. Come on—let me show you. What do you say you and me take a turn out on the floor? Can I borrow your lady, son?" he asked Doyle without giving Meehan a chance to answer.

"I don't think they allow dancing, Jake," Meehan said, laughing.

"Don't worry. The song will be over before the MPs get here—okay?" he said, looking at Doyle.

"Just make sure you bring her back, sir," Doyle said.

Meehan gave him a pointed, thanks-a-lot look, but she got up. The spontaneous dancing precipitated a round of applause. What Jake lacked in ability he made up for in enthusiasm—much to the approval of his buddies at the table, if not the entire restaurant.

Doyle kept his eyes on Meehan. She knew how to do this kind of dancing and she looked really *fine*. She was enjoying herself, too, he decided, regardless of where bagel boy might be at the moment. Watching, Doyle hoped. So he could see what he'd been dumb enough to turn loose.

When the song ended, Jake brought Meehan back to the table, delivering her into her chair and giving her a kiss on the cheek. To Doyle he offered a smart salute and left.

"Nice moves," Doyle said to Meehan.

She laughed. "Oh, sure. I haven't had an evening this wild since I was in nursing school."

"'Wild' is good sometimes," he said, waxing philosophical just for her benefit. "Trust me."

"Are you ready to go?" she asked, because the waitress was bringing the boxes of pie.

"I'm ready," he said, sending the money for the meal and the tip with the waitress on her little payment tray. He let Meehan carry the pie, and he didn't get up out of his chair as smoothly as he'd hoped. His legs were killing him, and he had to work hard to hide it.

"Shoulder," Meehan said, when they'd gone a few steps.

He didn't hesitate. He put his hand on her shoulder the way he had when he was trying to make it into her house, feeling her soft, warm skin under his fingers and bearing down hard with every step.

Eat your heart out, bagel boy, wherever you are.

"Wait or walk?" she asked when they were outside.

"Walk," he said, not because he thought he could make it to the car, but because he just didn't want to let go of her shoulder.

"Mrs. Bee's or ninety miles an hour down I-95?" she asked when he'd finally gotten himself in the car.

"Interstate," he said. "Crank up…the…music."

He leaned back and closed his eyes, losing himself in the pain and the sounds from 96.5 FM.

Oldie goldie music.

The kind he never listened to. The kind that went with the car, and maybe with his sudden not-so-jolly mood.

The words flew past him, like the lights of downtown Fayetteville and then the traffic on the interstate.

"Light my fire…"

Hell, yes. He needed his fire lit. He needed it *bad*.

"Love hurts…"

Now there's news.

He took a deep breath, fighting the pain in his legs more than the pain in his heart. He didn't know where they were going; he didn't care. Everything went by in a blur. Meehan was doing what little old Mrs. Bee asked her to do. Blowing the Thunderbird out.

Flying.

"The danger zone…"

Flying.

He could feel the wind in his face. Like jumping out of a C-130—with a sound track and no sensation of falling.

"Maggie Mae…"

The anthem for lovesick college boys who had it bad for an older woman.

"Maggie Mae.…"

Chapter Four

The church ladies were downstairs. Some of them, anyway. Not a big crowd, but enough of them for Doyle to want to keep out of the way. For once he had no inclination to hit them up for free refreshments. He just wanted to…

…hang around upstairs and be on the lookout for Meehan, he thought with a candidness he'd been avoiding for days. Ordinarily he didn't try to dodge the bullet when it came to knowing what was what, but there was just no getting around it. He hadn't seen or talked to her since their steak and beer outing, and it was becoming increasingly clear to him how much he wanted to.

He kept telling himself that he was only interested

in making sure she was all right. She had tried to maintain a certain level of indifference about her "dumped" status, but he knew better. He'd been front and center for that business of sitting in the rain. She'd taken the bagel guy's wordy exit hard.

Regardless of all that, he could recognize the truth of the situation. There was nothing mysterious going on here. He wanted to see her. He wanted to talk to her. He wanted to make her laugh, if he could. He wanted to know about her sisters and her uncle Patrick and who the kids were in the pictures she had sitting around.

And why a good-looking woman like her wasn't married.

But, for all his diligence, he'd somehow managed to miss all her comings and goings. He hadn't seen her leave for work, and he hadn't seen her come home—and not for lack of trying. For three days he'd been in the wrong place at the wrong time. He'd considered asking Mrs. Bee if she'd talked to Meehan, but ultimately he'd abandoned that plan. Rita Warren, the girl he seriously cared about, had just married another man. He should have learned some kind of lesson here. When it came to high-maintenance women, the last thing he needed was to get all entangled up in the personal problems of yet another one. He couldn't ask Mrs. Bee. The fewer people who knew what an idiot he was when it came to women the better.

Yesterday—oh, man, yesterday. When it came to idiotic behavior, he'd really outdone himself. He'd had a doctor's follow-up appointment, for which he'd come early and stayed late solely for the purpose of trying to track Meehan down at work. He just wanted to say hello, maybe see if she was interested in hearing what the doctor said—or whatever. He hadn't quite mapped out that part. Not that it mattered. She wasn't at her post, and he realized too late that he was getting entirely too many inquisitive looks for his comfort level. People who knew them both and were wondering what the hell Bugs Doyle wanted with Nurse Meehan.

And the thing was, he really didn't know what he wanted—beyond the obvious—or obvious to him, at any rate. He didn't think it would occur to her that he was even remotely thinking of her as a sex object. A few days ago it wouldn't have occurred to *him* that he was even remotely thinking of her as a sex object. There wasn't a chance in hell that it was reciprocal. As far as Meehan was concerned, he was some kind of hard-luck case, a pity pal she needed to feel sorry for and maybe stop and pat on the head now and then. He'd all but begged her to let him buy her a steak dinner. The thing about wanting to pay her back for the blanket wasn't exactly what he would call smooth. Of course, at the time he'd believed that was the reason. Now he…wasn't so sure.

Man, she should never have worn that dress, he thought. He would have been just fine with this whole thing if she'd just looked the way she always looked at the hospital. Official. In command. Tough and a little mean. No soft, bare shoulders and little

straps that kept falling off them, leaving him no al-
ternative but to think about putting them back where
they belonged. And no dresses he couldn't see
through but still managed to make him forget who
she was and who he was and why he shouldn't be
thinking what he was thinking.

She was a *good*-looking woman. For a long time,
he'd been traumatized in body, mind and spirit—but
he wasn't dead yet—as recent events proved beyond
a shadow of a doubt.

"There's nothing wrong with talking to her, damn
it," he said out loud. That shouldn't be a problem
for either of them, because he was absolutely certain—most of the time—that they had both enjoyed
the steak-and-beer evening. They were "comfortable" together. No expectations. No man-woman
games. Just "buds."

Sort of.

He maneuvered across the room until he could
look out the window. Again.

"Now what?" he said, because there was a car
in Meehan's driveway, one he recognized immediately. The boyfriend was back.

Doyle watched as the bagel guy walked purposefully across the patio to the back door, watched as
he rang the doorbell, watched as he went inside.

So.

That's that, then.

Meehan must have been expecting him or she
wouldn't have let him come right into the house like
that. The ease with which he made entry also sug-

gested that she wanted him there. She must have changed her mind after all about letting him feel guilty.

Doyle sighed heavily. There was no point standing by the window staring at Meehan's house like some horny teenage boy whose hormone-driven imagination didn't even come close to his reality. He'd go downstairs and stare at it—in spite of the fact that whatever was going on over there was none of his business.

He took the army shrink's advice and tried to identify the emotion he was feeling—the one that wasn't total aggravation.

Or lust.

Concern, he decided after a moment.

He was definitely concerned, in spite of the fact that he had no doubt she could take care of herself. He just didn't want that guy jerking Meehan around again.

But there was more to it than that, and he knew it. Yes, he was aggravated. Yes, he was concerned and on the high side lustful. But at the top of the list, incredibly, was…jealousy.

He was actually jealous, and where had *that* come from? Somehow his making that long, rainy and unwilling hike across the yard to see about her had translated into a certain sense of responsibility where she was concerned—like he had controlling interest in her welfare now.

Sir Galahad with a cane.

He'd come to her rescue—sort of. Now he felt responsible for her.

Very simple.

A distinct hazard for would-be Galahads everywhere.

He left his apartment and went painfully down the back stairs, the ultimate goal being pretty much the same as always—to get to the porch all in one piece. It was amazing to him that he could forget how much it was going to hurt from one time to the next. But then, if he could remember, he probably wouldn't go—unless the place was on fire.

It took everything he had to keep moving. At one particularly painful point, he had to mentally call up his old drill sergeant.

"You will persevere—soldier," he recited under his breath in a not-so-instant replay of his basic training days. "The thousands…and thousands who…have gone before…you…demand it! You will not 'try'! You will do! Failure is not an option! Hoo-ah!"

Hoo-ah! Too easy!

He made it to the swing eventually, but he had the shakes. He was hot and sweaty—but upright. Once again his old drill sergeant would be proud. He wiped his face a couple of times on the underside of his T-shirt, wondering idly what ever happened to the son of a bitch. Still somewhere scaring the hell of recruits, he supposed.

The church ladies were all in the front parlor. The downstairs windows were up because of Mrs. Bee's penchant for "natural" air-conditioning, and he could hear them plainly. They must have heard him, as well, because their voices dropped to whispers almost immediately. Whatever was going on in there, his arrival had put a crimp in it—big time.

But he was still too unsteady to effect a strategic withdrawal. Mrs. Bee and the girls were just going to have to work around him for the time being. He sat there, trying to stretch out the pain in his legs and not swear. He couldn't imagine what the church ladies could be doing that he shouldn't know about. After a time they apparently forgot to whisper.

"Do you think he would?" somebody asked.

"Oh, for heaven's sake, just ask him," somebody else said.

"No!" at least three voices responded.

"What would people say? I'm telling you right now, this ain't going to cause nothing but trouble and heartache," a different voice said. "What if it's not legal?"

"Well, *he'll* know. I'm not afraid to ask him—"

"No," he heard Mrs. Bee say. "*I'll* ask him."

He could hear the scraping of the dining room chairs Mrs. Bee would have dragged in for the women who couldn't get up from low, upholstered couches anymore—and then the mass exodus from the parlor. Before he could make a run for it, Mrs. Bee was at the screen door, clearly with a mission.

"Calvin," she said in her schoolteacher voice.

"Yes, ma'am," Doyle said, trying not to smile. Whatever it was, it was damned serious.

"I...we," she said, indicating the four little old ladies behind her, "need a—" she made a circle in the air with one hand "—little favor."

It took all of ten minutes for the cars to start arriving. The driveway was full, and one side of the street in front of the house.

The word was definitely out.

Doyle sat on the swing to recover from the mission, trying not to grin. He'd never heard such giggling. A sudden chorus of little-old lady squeals rose from the parlor, a good indication that the newest arrivals must have just been apprised of the situation.

"Oh, pooh," somebody said. "I had titties every bit that good when I was that age."

"Lula Mae!" several voices said.

"Well, I did!" Lula Mae insisted.

I better get out of here, Doyle thought, chuckling to himself. Somebody was going to end up embarrassed before this thing was all over, and more than likely it was going to be him.

He hobbled out into the backyard, eventually sitting down at the cement picnic table near the sagging grapevine—well out of the traffic pattern. A stand of pine trees grew along the edge of the property. He could smell them. Pine—and honeysuckle—and dry earth in need of rain.

He occupied himself by looking around.

At the sky.

At the wasps maneuvering in and out of the grape vine.

He didn't look toward Meehan's house, regardless of how easy it would have been to do so. Without warning, a sudden wave of longing washed over him—for what he wasn't exactly sure.

For his old, precrash self?

For Rita?

Maybe for Pop Doyle's farm in Georgia—which was probably a parking lot by now.

He had been happy there when he was growing up. Until Pop died, it had been the one place he'd always wanted to come back to. He would arrive unannounced after every overseas tour of duty, loaded down with souvenirs and embellished stories of his military adventures abroad. The farm was where he had learned that working hard was a lot better than feeling sorry for himself and that some people would love him and some people wouldn't, regardless of their blood ties—and there wasn't a damn thing he could do about it.

His mind went briefly to his mother and his only sister, Nina, in Florida. It had been months since he'd talked to either one of them. Nina had surprised him by coming to see him in the hospital shortly after he'd been hurt—which only served as an indicator of how really bad off he was. No way would she have come if somebody hadn't told her he was dying—and even then it was iffy.

His mother had called a few times while he was on Meehan's ward—which was likely the result of somebody she knew asking her how her poor, multifractured, somewhat crispy paratrooper son was, and her realizing that, for the sake of appearances if nothing else, she ought to at least ask.

He couldn't deny that he and his mother and sister essentially stayed out of each other's way, but he no longer blamed them for what could only be described as a heartfelt indifference. He had been born late in his mother's marriage, a change-of-life baby. The last thing she'd wanted was another kid, especially a rowdy male child, and her solution had been to dump him into his equally unwilling sister's lap. Both women had had their own individual game plans for their lives, and come hell, high water or a surprise addition to the family, they'd stuck to them.

He'd gotten through it, though, essentially raising himself until he had a big enough run-in with the law to get sent to live with his Georgian grandparents—and he would be grateful to whoever had come up with that solution until his dying day. He finally had a place to belong, and Pop had taken the time to try to explain the women in his family as kindly as he could. "Them two wells is dirt dry, boy," he said in another of his homespun correlations. "And you can keep going to them and going to them until hell freezes over—but you ain't going to get what you need from neither one of them. And after so long a time, you begin to look like a damn fool for trying."

If Calvin "Bugs" Doyle had been any good at all for Rita Warren, it had been in helping her see the truth of that principle when it came to her own careless family. Thanks to Pop, both of them were able to get a handle on things, to understand one simple truth: people are the way they are, and you can keep knocking yourself out trying to change them or you can move on. He was trying to do that right now—with her.

Move on.

He closed his eyes, feeling the summer heat rise up around him. He was still hot and sweaty.

And tired.

Every now and then, enough of a breeze stirred to make the tall pine trees creak and sigh. Thunder rumbled in the distance. Maybe it would rain, he thought. And if it did, maybe he could sleep—a good sleep with no dreams and no pain. Wouldn't that be something? He hadn't slept like that since he'd crashed on the couch at Meehan's house.

A small cracking sound made him open his eyes again. Meehan was coming through the hedge toward where he was sitting. The boyfriend stood waiting impatiently in the driveway next to his car, and he kept looking toward the street, as if he expected yet another little old lady to arrive, one who would have the audacity to park where she shouldn't and box him in.

Meehan wasn't all dressed up this time. She looked more like the old Meehan, her hair twisted up and caught in a big barrette, her clothes baggy and not showing off anything. He realized immediately that it didn't matter. He had an excellent memory of what she looked like under them.

"Bugs," she called with some alarm. "What's wrong? Did something happen? Is Mrs. Bee okay?"

"Nothing…yes…and yes," he said.

"Well, what?" she asked, looking over her shoulder at all the cars.

"I bought the church ladies a girlie magazine."

"You what!"

"You heard me," he said.

"What kind of girlie magazine?"

"The under-the-counter, wrapped-in-plastic kind."

"Why on earth did you do that?"

"Why? Because they made me, that's why. One minute I'm sitting on the swing minding my own business—sort of—and the next minute Thelma and Louise is out of the motor pool and we're all wheeling down the highway heading for the nearest dirty book store—and you can stop grinning about anytime now."

She tried…but she didn't make it. "Now wait. They *made* you go buy them a girlie magazine."

"Correct."

"*Why?*"

"Well…see…there's this one church lady that's a royal pain in the butt. She treats them all like bastards at the wedding and they're way tired of it—"

"Pitty-Pat McCall."

"That would be her. Well, word got out some relative of Miss Pitty-Pat's is in the magazine."

"Posing, you mean?"

"Roger that," he said, and Meehan laughed out loud.

"And they're all in there looking at it?"

"That would be my guess."

"Are you telling me the truth?" she asked with a suspicion that was certainly justified.

"You think I could make up something this wacky?"

"Actually, no," she said, laughing again. "It just doesn't sound like Mrs. Bee."

"Yeah, well, we all have our limits."

"So what are they going to do? Are they going to show Pitty-Pat the magazine? Or at least tell her they've seen it?"

"Nah," he said. He picked a pine needle off the picnic table, twirled it between his thumb and forefinger for a second, then tossed it aside. "Mrs. Bee's got too much class for that. They took a vote. They're not going to say anything one way or the other."

"But the reign of terror is over, right?"

"Damn straight. So," he said, glancing toward where the boyfriend stood waiting. "What's new?"

"Are you doing all right?" she asked instead of answering.

"Are you?" he countered.

"I will be," she said.

"Me, too," he assured her—when he was certain that neither one of them believed a word of it. In fact, he thought maybe they were both trying too hard.

"How have you been sleeping?" she asked next, watching him closely. He could practically see her morphing from Mrs. Bee's concerned neighbor into the on-duty nurse.

"About like usual," he said vaguely.

"Meaning?"

He didn't answer. He looked into her eyes. She let him.

And let him.

Damn, Meehan, don't do that.

He didn't look away—couldn't have if he'd wanted to. He could sense a kind of sadness in her, a wistfulness, a *need* he couldn't identify, but one he knew she would never admit. It wasn't sexual— and yet it was. It left him unsettled and—

"Katherine!" the boyfriend suddenly called.

"I've got to run," she said, turning to go. "Tell Mrs. Bee to hang on to that magazine. I'm coming over to see it."

"I'd wait until the crowd clears," he called after her. "There are some bawdy old ladies in there. You wouldn't believe the things I've heard!"

She kept going, dismissing his remark with a laugh.

So what's wrong, Meehan? he thought, watching her go.

Maybe he'd been mistaken, he suddenly decided. Maybe she was just tired or something. She wouldn't take up with the boyfriend again if she didn't want to. That was the bottom line here.

Doyle could see him staring in their direction, *wondering*—just the way he himself had wondered earlier when he spotted the silver car in Meehan's drive.

"That's that, then," he said out loud when she got into the bagel guy's car and they drove away.

He continued to sit at the picnic table for what seemed a long time. He felt rested now, up for the return trip.

To nowhere.

He didn't want to go back upstairs to his apartment. And he couldn't hang with the church ladies when they were passing that magazine around.

He suddenly smiled to himself. What a day. Mrs. Bee should have charged admission.

The wind was picking up. The pines began to sway and sigh. He could smell the rain coming, and if he started now, he might make it to the house before the storm hit.

When he reached the porch, he headed for the back stairs. He could hear the ladies in the parlor. They were still having a good time. He could almost feel sorry for old Pitty-Pat. He wondered if she'd ever know how it was she came to lose her throne. He'd had occasion to see the woman in action the day the church ladies had dragged him into the parlor for cake and punch. He supposed that her regime had been on a downward slide even then, because she clearly hadn't wanted the likes of him there.

Mrs. Bee must have overridden the woman's authority. The kingdom had been restless even then.

His mind suddenly went to Meehan. He didn't understand the bagel guy's return—but then he didn't have to. And he didn't have to worry about her anymore. She'd seemed happy enough—except for when he'd looked into her eyes, and that might have been his imagination. The love-life situation with the bagel guy must be going her way, or she wouldn't have gone off with him.

He managed to get upstairs without any major pain events. He ate a peanut butter sandwich and drank some cold tea he had in a glass jar in the refrigerator. Then he watched television. The news. The weather.

And he was very careful not to go looking out the window to see if Meehan had come back home.

He realized at some point that the rainstorm he'd come inside to escape had never materialized. Sometime after nineteen-hundred, he heard the phone in the downstairs hall ringing and then Mrs. Bee calling him from the foyer.

"Calvin, that was a Specialist Will Baron," she said when he hobbled to the head of the stairs. "He just wanted you to know that he's your COC person—I think that's right. COC. He left a number for you to call him if you need anything. I'll leave it right here by the phone."

"Thanks, Mrs. Bee."

He hobbled back into his apartment and closed

the door, trying to remember if he knew the guy. He did, he decided. A guy from Arizona, maybe Native American. He had relatives around here some-where—a bunch of the guys from the unit had gone home with him to eat once. He was a…medic.

And Meehan's heavy hand was all over this little gesture. COC. Chain of Concern. The Army's unof-ficial answer to soldiers in distress. Well, he wasn't in as much distress now as he had been, he was happy to say. He was just…

Too damn nosy for his own good.

And maybe this concern thing he had with Meehan was a two-way street. They were both so busy wor-rying about each other's emotional welfare, it was a wonder they didn't knock each other down.

He was tired suddenly, sleepy, but he didn't go to bed. He sat in the chair in front of the television instead. He dropped off almost immediately, and he woke up on the floor.

"What…?"

"Lie still," someone said.

Meehan?

"Meehan…what…is it?" he said, trying to under-stand, trying to sit up.

"Wait!" she said. "Let me see if you've hurt yourself."

He stopped struggling and closed his eyes. He could feel her hands moving over him. When he opened his eyes again, he was still lying on the floor, and Meehan was kneeling beside him. Her hair was all wet.

"Is it raining?" he asked crazily.

"No. Mrs. Bee got me out of the shower."

"Mrs. Bee?"

"Yes. She heard you—she was worried. Does anything hurt? More than usual, I mean."

"I...don't understand," he said, trying to sit up again. This time Meehan let him. "What happened?"

"You were yelling."

"Yelling? What did I say?"

"You thought you were on the Black Hawk," she said quietly.

He took a deep breath. The Black Hawk. The goddamn Black Hawk. He could hear it suddenly, smell it, feel the heat. He realized that his hands were shaking, and he clenched his fists so she wouldn't see.

"Then she heard you fall, but she couldn't get the door open—so she came and got me."

"How the hell did you get in?" he asked, because he realized that he had been lying up against the door.

She smiled. "I went out the window at the end of the hall and I came across the roof. You should have seen me. I was great."

He couldn't help but smile in return. "I'll bet."

The smile immediately faded, and he sat there with his head bowed.

"Are you ready to get up?"

"What? Yeah...yeah..."

But he made no effort to do so. "Mrs. Bee came and got you?"

"Yes. She's very hard to say no to."

"Tell me about it," he said. He gave a sudden sharp exhalation of breath. "They're supposed to get better—the nightmares."

"They will," she said. "When you forgive yourself."

"Forgive myself? For what? I wasn't flying the damn thing."

"For surviving," she said. Her voice was still quiet.

Quiet.

And so *sure*.

"And you would know all about that, I guess," he said.

She didn't answer him.

"So what are you going to do now? Tell me everything happens for a reason?"

"Maybe it does," she said.

He made a short derisive sound, but he was suddenly faced with a different, more pressing problem—the overwhelming urge to bawl. Like a little kid—only he never cried much when he was a kid. He'd just sucked it up and gone on his not-so-merry way.

He didn't dare look at her. He turned away and tried to get to his feet. Her hand came out to help him at just the right moment, efficient and nonintrusive. Something she'd no doubt learned from years of practice. She handed him his cane.

"I'm okay now," he said, struggling to walk to the bed. Meehan went with him, but she made no attempt to help. He sat down heavily on the edge of the mattress.

He could feel her looking at him, assessing.

"Then I'll be going," she said after a moment.

"Hey," he said when she was halfway across the room.

She looked back at him.

"Sorry I interrupted your shower."

"No problem."

"Hey," he said again when she opened the door. "Maybe we could go get another steak and beer sometime. Or something."

She gave him a small, sad smile and shook her head. "No."

The no-frills, no-discussion, no-chance-of-misunderstanding answer.

No.

Chapter Five

She probably thought I wasn't with it enough to know what I was asking.

It wouldn't be hard for her to make that mistake. He'd been asleep. He'd apparently been yelling, and he'd definitely been falling—he had the bruises to prove it. So what else would she think but that his brain had been temporarily scrambled?

The only solution as far as he could see was to just do it again—when he was in better shape and she would *know* he was in better shape and not think he didn't have a clue about what he was saying.

Sounded like a plan.

He went outside to the backyard when he thought Meehan would be getting home from work, taking up his post by the grapevine.

He waited.

And waited.

He had to suffer a lot of insect pests of one kind or another in the time it took her to show—clearly he was the specialty of the day. When she pulled into her drive, he stood up and walked as casually as he could in her direction. The only problem was that his casual gait looked a lot like his I'm-about-to-fall-on-my-face one. Thankfully, she saw him at some point and walked to meet him.

"Hey," he said when she was close enough. "I've got a question."

"Go ahead," she said, and it occurred to him that she probably thought it was about something medical.

"Are you and the bagel guy on or off?"

She seemed about to say something, but apparently she thought better of it, probably deciding—given their history—that she'd save herself a lot of aggravation in the long run if she just bit the bullet and answered him.

"Off," she said.

Hot damn!

"Okay," he said. "So what do you think about you and me going out to eat again sometime?"

"The same thing I thought last night. No."

"Why not?"

"Why not? What is the matter with you? You should be going out with your—" she hunted for a word "—military associates. Get busy and make some new friends. Or better yet, you should find yourself some nice girl to go places with.''

''I could do that,'' he assured her. ''But I haven't got the strength.''

''You haven't got the strength,'' she repeated— as if she'd *heard* him just fine, but *buying* it was something else again.

''Right. See, if I go hang out with somebody from the unit, I got to be tough all the time—show them Bugs Doyle is one more steely-eyed, badass military man, and he can take it. If I go out with some girl, not only do I have to be tough, I have to be suave, too. You know how much work it takes to be tough *and* suave?''

''I haven't got a clue,'' she assured him.

''I didn't think so. I'm better than I was, but I'm just not up for all that stuff yet. I don't need a nice girl. I need a—''

''Baby-sitter,'' she finished for him.

''No,'' he said pointedly. ''I need a friend—a bud. See, if *we* go out together, I don't have to be bothered with keeping up my image. If I hurt, I can say so. If I'm all down about Rita, I can say so. And you won't care. Same goes for you. I know about the bagel guy, so you can be however you want to be, too, because we don't have any secrets. I thought we had a pretty good time the other night. I did, anyway. Going out with you was a big relief, and I wouldn't mind going again. That's all. See?''

''Yes.''

"So you'll go?"

"No," she said. "But that was a nice try," she added. "You might even say 'suave.' Tell Mrs. Bee I'll be over to see the magazine soon."

She walked away, and he stared after her until she got inside.

Well, that went pretty well, he thought. She didn't threaten to report him to his commanding officer, at least.

He hobbled back to the house, going in through the kitchen instead of around to be back stairs. The telephone was on a table in the wide hall, and he toyed with the idea of calling his COC contact. For what, he didn't know. He could think of something, he supposed—if he hadn't still been occupied with Meehan and her civil but firm rebuff.

She's just not getting this, he thought.

And he was going to end up on the six o'clock news for stalking, if he wasn't careful.

He stood in the hall for a moment, then decided to hobble into the parlor. Mrs. Bee's bookshelves were in there, and she'd said on more than one occasion that he could take a look and help himself. At the time, he distinctly remembered thinking that he wished the offer had extended to the downstairs refrigerator.

She had a lot of books, essentially her own private Bee Library. He stood holding on to a shelf and reading the titles, finally taking down a photographic history of World War I. He flipped through the pages, looking at the many pictures of no-man's-land and the trenches and reading the captions.

Hell of a way to fight a war, he thought.

He put the book back and pulled out a thin red one with gold lettering. World War II—the history of the 963rd Field Artillery. There were a number of photographs in it, as well—men in little groups mostly.

He moved to one of the dining room chairs left in the church ladies' "war room" and sat down. He read for a time, then closed the book and sat thinking of the movie, *Saving Private Ryan* and the fact that maybe he wasn't as brave as those men had been. He wondered if Meehan had been to see it, and if so, what she thought of it. He could always ask—

"Calvin?" Mrs. Bee said in the doorway. "Can I help you find something?"

"Ah…no, Mrs. Bee. Well, maybe. Have you got any books by John…something that starts with a *G*. Some kind of 'saga.'"

"Galsworthy? *The Forsyte Saga?*"

"That's it."

"It's up there on the top shelf. Those three big books side by side, next to the end."

Three books?

"Okay, Mrs. Bee. Thanks."

He had to work to get them, but he brought all three down. He was pretty sure Mrs. Bee wouldn't have any idea that his interest had been sparked by *her* remark about his reminding her of Michael Mont, and he couldn't *not* look at them after she had been kind enough not to ask what in the world he wanted with them—not when it was obvious to him that he had stumbled on to some seriously highbrow books here. They still had the book jackets on them, for one thing. Interesting, readable books never did, in his experience. Mrs. Bee had to know that this wasn't his usual reading material, but she acted as if it was, and he appreciated it.

He skimmed over the blurbs and then began thumbing through the pages, trying to spot the name Michael Mont, until he ultimately decided that the middle volume might be the one.

He used to read a lot, especially when he was overseas. Nothing like this, of course. Cold War and spy things mostly, if he could get his hands on them. He hadn't read much since the helicopter crash. He hadn't been able to, and it had alarmed him enough to obliquely mention it to one of his doctors. He'd been relieved to learn that it wasn't some kind of brain damage, as he'd feared, but ''a decreased ability to concentrate due to post traumatic stress.'' Fortunately he'd been able to concentrate long enough to read that in the doctor's notes—upside down.

Post traumatic stress.

Maybe that was getting better—if he didn't count the recent nightmare. He still couldn't remember what he'd been dreaming about. He didn't want to remember it.

He picked up all three volumes of the saga, juggling them along as he dragged the dining room chair closer to the bay window where the lace curtains were billowing outward. Then he sat down in the cross breeze and began reading.

British guy, he thought after a moment. World War I vet.

Okay.

He'd been peacekeeping with British soldiers. He could hang with this.

He kept reading, wading through the drawing room conversations. It was kind of like going to a party where everybody else knew each other. Not that something like that had ever fazed him. Even when he was a kid, Pop Doyle had always said he had never met a stranger. And he hadn't, so he kept reading, kept absorbing information until he could form some kind of opinion as to why Mrs. Bee thought he was like this Michael Mont. So far, he didn't have a clue.

He heard Mrs. Bee go out. After a few moments he heard her backing out the drive. He smiled to himself. That was some car. She must be going somewhere special if she was letting Thelma and Louise out on the road again so soon.

He continued to read, certain now of at least one fact. Michael Mont was pretty far gone on somebody named Fleur. The reason became obvious after a time. Fleur was another high-maintenance woman—in his opinion, the only kind worth having. Something was seriously wrong with a guy who could be happy with a doormat.

At one point he decided he wanted more background on this relationship, and he closed the book he was reading and picked up the first volume, thumbing through the pages again to look for Michael Mont's name.

He found it after a time and began to read, but the most he was able to figure out was that Mont was kind of funny looking in the ear department.

Not exactly a flattering thought.

He looked up because the front screen door slammed. Mrs. Bee came and stood in the doorway again.

"Calvin?" she said after a moment. She was frowning.

"Something wrong, Mrs. Bee?" he asked.

"You were talking to Katie earlier."

"Yes, ma'am."

"Does she...know about that magazine?"

"Mrs. Bee, everybody on the Eastern Seaboard knows about that magazine," he said with as much truth as teasing. "Why?"

"Oh," she said, still frowning. "I just didn't want to make her...uncomfortable."

He looked at her, not understanding. Meehan was nothing if not broad-minded. If anything, she'd gotten a kick out of Operation Spread Eagle. She hadn't been the least bit uncomfortable.

"I don't think you have to worry about that, Mrs. Bee," he said.

"I just don't want to remind her of her own problems. I wouldn't upset that sweet girl for the world. I just wouldn't."

"I don't understand," he said—because he still didn't.

"Well, she was so sick," Mrs. Bee said, as if that explained everything.

He waited for her to elaborate. She didn't.

"Meehan said to tell you she'd be coming over to see the magazine."

"Oh, no!" Mrs. Bee said, clearly alarmed.

"Mrs. Bee...it's okay. She's not going to think—"

"Calvin, that magazine is just going to remind her of a very bad time."

"What bad time?" he asked, because he was beginning to get a little alarmed himself.

Mrs. Bee looked at him, but she didn't say anything.

"Tell me, Mrs. Bee."

"I shouldn't have said anything—"

"Mrs. Bee, I like Meehan. It's better if I know what's going on, don't you think? You need to tell me, so I don't go saying or doing something even more stupid than usual. You know how we are, right? Hunt the hill and all that?"

Mrs. Bee sighed. "She had cancer," she said after a moment. "Three years ago."

Cancer.

Doyle tried to get his mind around the word. It was the last thing he expected to hear. His worst-case scenario had been that maybe she'd been hard-up for money at some point in her life, and she'd posed like Pitty-Pat What's-Her-Name's relative.

"In her...breast," Mrs. Bee said. "She ought not be looking at a magazine like that. It's just going to remind her. Lula Mae was right. This magazine thing is just going to cause trouble and heartache."

Doyle sat staring at the Galsworthy book, fighting off questions like, How bad was it? This wasn't something he should be discussing with his landlady. Even he could recognize that.

When he looked up again, Mrs. Bee was still standing in the doorway.

"I'm sure you'll know what to do, Calvin."

"*Me?*" he said, startled. "About what?"

"The *magazine,* Calvin."

"Now wait a minute, Mrs. Bee—"

But Mrs. Bee was already in retreat.

"Mrs. Bee!" he called after her.

"You're a good boy, Calvin," he heard her call from somewhere deep in the house.

"I'm not *that* good," he said under his breath.

So what did Mrs. Bee want him to do? Ditch the magazine for her so she wouldn't have to fib about it when Meehan came over? He didn't even know where the damn thing was. He sat for a moment longer, then struggled to get to his feet. With considerable difficulty, he put Michael Mont and Fleur back on the shelf. He no longer had the time nor the inclination to worry about them.

In the process of dragging the dining room chair back to where he found it, he looked out the bay window. He could see Meehan on her patio, doing something with a bag of dirt and some pots and petunias.

I like her, he thought, watching her work. A lot. And that means...?

He knew what it meant. It meant that he was standing here in his dented-up, not-so-shining armor, ready to ride to the rescue. The only thing wrong with this picture was that he suddenly felt that it wasn't Meehan who needed rescuing. It was him. He was getting to know her, and he didn't want anything to happen to her—for his sake.

He took a deep breath. He should just go upstairs and forget all this. He would do exactly that—if he had the sense God gave a turnip. He began walking, across the room and into the wide center hallway. The ceiling fan waffled overhead, echoing his own indecision. He stood for a moment in the current of air. He could hear Mrs. Bee in the kitchen. He could go in there. He could go up the stairs. But, instead of doing either, he began to make his way toward the front door. He kept going, out onto the porch, down the steps and across the yard.

Meehan had to hear him coming, but she didn't look up.

"Let me guess," she said when he reached the edge of the patio, still not looking at him. "Another question."

"No. Yes," he abruptly decided. Her portable phone lay conspicuously on a nearby lounge chair. Handy, in case the boyfriend decided to call.

What the hell.

She put a handful of plastic foam packing "peanuts" in the bottom of a flower pot for drainage. Some of them stuck to her fingers, then blew across the patio in a sudden breeze. She didn't try to chase them down. She just kept fiddling with the petunias.

"I want to know why you won't go out with me," he said bluntly.

"I'm older than you are," she answered—as if she'd expected to have to go through this again, and she'd gotten her big guns all ready.

"Right," he said. "Not much we can do about that."

"The age difference is significant," she said next—still without looking at him.

"Not to me it isn't. Is it just me in particular, or do you have age requirements for all your friends?"

She didn't answer him. She stuck another red petunia plant in the pot, then a white one, then carefully began pouring potting soil around them with a bent paper cup.

"The thing is," he went on. "I like you. And I think you like me—so what's the problem?"

"Bugs, I really don't want to have this conversation."

"The thing is," he said again, anyway. "I can't do a damn thing about when I was born, right? There's no point in either one of us getting all bothered about it—"

"Bugs—"

"Now wait. Let me finish here. If you don't want to go out with me because I've got it all wrong and you *don't* like me and you *don't* enjoy my company…well, I'm okay with that, and I won't bother you. But if you don't want to go out with me just because of the cancer thing, that's something else again."

She finally looked up at him.

"Mrs. Bee told me," he said.

"What? That I'm a breast cancer survivor?"

"Yeah. I'm sorry."

"Sorry I survived?" she said with a flippancy he didn't think she felt.

"Sorry you had to go through all that."

She was staring into his eyes. Once again he could feel her trying to decide whether or not he meant it. It was becoming increasingly clear to him that Meehan must have had to deal with a lot of liars in her time.

She abruptly looked down at the pot and began packing the dirt around the petunias with more force than necessary. Another breeze came through, this one strong enough to stir the wind chimes—glass, brass and bamboo. He could smell the fragrance of lemon again, and any other time he would have asked her about it.

"The other day," he said. "When you were sitting out in the rain—"

"I told him," she interrupted, reaching for a new pot.

"I...guess he didn't take it too well."

"He didn't take it well at all. I...misjudged him. I thought I'd learned enough from past mistakes to be able to tell at least a little something about a man's character. I was wrong."

"Well, he did come back—more than once."

"I told you. He didn't want to feel guilty. He also didn't much like the idea that I might be taking up with you."

"What's wrong with me?" he asked, grinning. "Besides the obvious, that is—"

He stopped because she was smiling.

All right!

Doyle, the Magnificent, has done it again!

"This doesn't have to be a big deal, Meehan. What I'm saying is if you want to go someplace and you don't particularly want to go by yourself—"

"I don't think I'm going to need any girlie magazines."

"—I'm your man," he finished as if she hadn't interrupted.

She sighed and didn't say anything—which he

supposed was better than having her throw a flower pot.

"So what do you think?" he asked, because he was ever the one to push his luck.

"I think you want to get into my pants," she said bluntly, and he laughed out loud. This was some woman here—high maintenance and then some.

"Your pants are safe," he said, still grinning. "I swear."

She wasn't even close to believing him.

"Really," he said, trying not to grin and not quite making it. "Anyway, you could outrun me."

"That's true," she said, going back to her flowers.

"So what do you say?"

"Nothing."

Nothing is better than *no,* he thought.

"But you'll keep it in mind."

"I'll keep it in mind," she said.

"Great!"

"Now, go away."

"Okay," he said.

"You're an idiot. You know that," she added.

"I've…had my suspicions," he confessed. "So how's Uncle Patrick?"

"Uncle Patrick?"

"Yeah. You remember him. The one you were going to have to yell at."

"I'm still going to have to yell at him."

"Too bad," he said, looking around at the sound

of a car. He didn't recognize this one—it wasn't the bagel guy, at any rate. The car skidded to a stop in the driveway, and a young woman got out, a younger version of Meehan. She had a little boy with her.

Meehan gave a quiet sigh. "Now what?" she said under her breath.

They watched the young woman struggle to get the boy out of the back seat. Meehan walked forward, and Doyle went with her, trailing along behind. He had every intention of going back through the hedge where he belonged. He'd had too many family dramas of his own to want to get tangled up in somebody else's.

"Do you know anything about kids?" Meehan stopped to ask him on the way. "Do you think you can keep Scottie occupied for a little bit, if his mother is all upset?"

"No problem," he heard himself say without the slightest hesitation.

"I'd appreciate it."

"No problem," he said again.

She looked at him for a moment, then went to help. The young woman had apparently given up. She stood by the car, and Doyle realized that she was crying. He had to step back when she hurried past him toward Meehan's patio, completely oblivious to anyone or anything in her path. She didn't go inside the house. She abruptly sat down on the lounge chair, upsetting the portable phone. It clattered onto the brick patio. She made no attempt to pick it up.

He waited while Meehan got the little boy out of the car. She walked with him to where Doyle stood, holding him by the hand.

"This is Scottie," she said. "Scottie, this is Bugs Doyle. He's a soldier."

"A real one?" Scottie wanted to know. In his other hand he was holding a small, red velvet bag with a drawstring.

"A real one," Meehan assured him.

"Can he drive a tank?"

"He jumps out of airplanes."

"Why?"

"Why?" Meehan asked, directing the question to the source.

"So I can get to the ground without having to wait for the plane," Doyle said. Then, "Hey, Scottie. What have you got there?"

"Rocks," Scottie said.

"Can I see?"

The boy looked up at Meehan to see if she had any objections, then let go of her hand.

"Okay," he said. "But you can't know. I have to tell you, okay?"

"Right," Doyle said. "Can we sit down first?"

"Yes," Scottie advised him.

"Over there?" Doyle pointed to Mrs. Bee's picnic table.

"Yes."

Scottie led the way. "You can't walk fast," he said.

"No."

"You got hurt legs."

"Yeah."

"I got a hurt leg one time. Aunt Kate fixed it. I bet she can fix you."

"I bet she can, too."

He made a point of sitting on the far side of the table so he could see Meehan and—if he wanted to make a wild guess—her sister. Scottie hopped up on the stone bench and dumped his rocks out on the table. The kid had a nice collection—polished stones mostly, some fool's gold, a few pieces of road gravel.

"Cool," Doyle pronounced them. "Where did you get them?"

"Dan Nicholas Park," he said. "Uncle Patrick took me to them. They got a merry-go-round. And a train. And rocks." He rubbed his nose with the heel of his hand. "And bees," he added.

"You have to watch out for bees," Doyle said.

"Yeah," Scottie said with a little giggle in his voice.

"So what's this one," Doyle asked, pointing to, but being careful not to actually touch, a small ragged piece of turquoise.

"Chewing bubble-gum sharing rock," Scottie said solemnly.

"Wow," Doyle said, glancing over the boy's

head. His mother was really crying now. He could see Meehan reach out to put her hand on her arm.

"And this one?" he asked

"Green garden kinder rock."

"What about that one?" he asked, pointing to the fool's gold.

"Golden crispin," Scottie said without hesitation, and Doyle smiled, wondering where he'd gotten his creative rock names.

"You really know your rocks."

"Yes," Scottie said. "My mommy's crying."

"Yeah," Doyle said. "I think she is."

The boy looked at him sharply, as if the truth was the last thing he expected. He turned his red velvet bag upside down as if to clear out any rock that might have remained.

"I have to stay over here." It wasn't quite a question, but Doyle answered it, anyway.

"Yeah. For right now. We'll be okay. Don't worry."

"I'm not going to cry," he said.

Doyle didn't know what to say to that, or even if the comment was meant for him. The boy looked up at him.

"I don't want my mommy to be sad."

"Well, I think your aunt Kate can make her feel better—like she made you feel better when you hurt your leg."

"Aunt Kate can make her feel better," Scottie repeated. He gave a little sigh.

"Tell me about the rest of your rocks, okay?"

Scottie went back to naming his collection. When he reached the "white recklin rock," Doyle saw the boy's mother hide her face in her hands, but by the time he'd identified a "blue tiger falgon" and a "purple shark seaweed," she seemed to have gotten control of herself—which was a good thing, because they were running out of rocks.

But the two women continued to talk. Meehan was obviously listening—and not particularly liking what she heard. Doyle knew her well enough to recognize the body language. It was something on the order of when he was still a patient on her ward, and she found out Rita had smuggled him an ice-cold beer in her purse. The fact that he hadn't drunk the thing made no difference whatsoever.

He realized suddenly that Scottie was looking at him.

"How long has it been since you washed these things?" he asked, relying on his own boyhood memory of how much he liked to play in water.

"Forty days and nights," Scottie said, and Doyle grinned.

"That long, huh? In that case, we better find some water."

Thankfully, it was a short trip to the nearest outside water spigot. It stuck up out of the ground, not too far from the driveway, handy for washing cars and watering Mrs. Bee's little patch of tomato plants.

He was allowed to hold the rocks in his hands while Scottie turned the water on. And off. And on again. They both got wet, but it couldn't be helped. Meehan had asked him to keep the kid occupied, not dry.

They carried the rocks back to the picnic table for a meticulous one-by-one, hand drying—with the tail ends of their T-shirts. Scottie kept up a running conversation, admiring what he imagined was a decided improvement in the appearance of his collection.

When the drying was done, they made up new, off-the-wall rock names as Scottie dropped each one back into the red velvet sack. The kid had a sense of humor, for all his worry about his mother. It didn't take much effort on Doyle's part to make him giggle.

Doyle looked up at one point to see Meehan heading in their direction. The sister had disappeared, he supposed, into the house.

"Come on, Scottie," Meehan said, holding out her hand. "Time to go."

"Is my mommy happy now?"

"She will be when you get there," Meehan said, lifting him down to the ground. "Tell Bugs bye."

"Bye," he said. "We can play some more later."

Meehan gave him a look, one Doyle had no problem at all deciphering. It was: See? I told you you were too young.

He grinned—and kept his mouth shut for once.

Meehan looked back as she walked away with Scottie in tow, mouthing the words, Thank you.

You're welcome, he thought. You are welcome.

He eventually took up his usual perch on the porch swing, and he sat there a long time, thinking about Meehan and whether he'd gained any ground here or not.

Probably not. But he didn't think he'd lost any, either.

He was just about to go inside when Meehan and her sister came out of the house.

"I'll be back to get Scottie in a hour. I promise," the sister said. Then, "Don't look at me like that! I have to see him! I love him with all my heart, Kate!"

"And you're stupid with all of your head," Meehan said.

He couldn't hear what she said next, but clearly she didn't hold back with family any more than she did with overzealous paratroopers.

He had no idea what the situation was here, but from what he did know, he could only come to one conclusion:

Poor old Scottie.

Chapter Six

Mrs. Bee was definitely on a trip down memory lane. She'd been listening to big band music all afternoon—some of which he recognized from having lived with grandparents. At the moment, a girl singer was doing a torchy rendition of ''More Than You Know.''

Mrs. Bee was also baking. Ordinarily, she took a nap in the afternoon, but not today. Man, the smells that were coming up from the kitchen. Apple pie, he thought. He couldn't remember the last time he'd had homemade apple pie—not since his grandmother had died, two weeks before Christmas when he was eighteen. After the funeral Pop had been determined to have the house decorated the way she always did—the red cedar Christmas tree hung with all kinds of kid-made ornaments and crammed into a corner of the living room, the multicolored lights strung across the front porch. But there were no kitchen smells. He and Pop couldn't manage that. By the next Christmas, he had graduated from high school and had joined the army.

No more homemade apple pie. Life as he knew it was over.

He'd forgotten how much he missed it.

So far, he hadn't made the effort to get downstairs to see exactly what was going on. His best guess was that the church ladies were about to ride again—this time well provisioned. It was probably time for the church's famous chicken pie supper, and Mrs. Bee was manning the desserts.

For the last two days he'd been trying to keep a low profile—so he wouldn't get roped into doing anything else unexpected. Little old church ladies, he was beginning to understand, were not all that predictable. There was still the matter of the notorious magazine, for one thing. Besides that, if he made the trip downstairs, he might be tempted to keep right on moving and go push his luck with Meehan. Restraining his well-honed inclination to take charge of the situation wasn't easy. He'd clearly found his misplaced audacity again, and he wanted to know if she was upset with him. He especially wanted to know about when she was sick, how bad it was and if she was okay now. She looked okay. She looked better than okay.

He could ask, of course—and probably would have a few days ago. It wasn't just his innate, cat-killing curiosity that made him so bold about making inquiries. It was his ongoing quest to understand the people around him. His emotional survival depended on it, just as much as his physical survival had once depended on his ability to go outside his food chain.

Or he was permanently stuck in Maslow's Hierarchy of Needs. Number five. The one he'd missed on the final exam.

"The need to know and understand."

He smiled to himself, surprised that he remembered even that much of the college course he'd taken in his better, precrash days.

But in spite of the motivation, he had to bide his time and stay out of Meehan's way for now. He'd said what he wanted—needed—to say, and that was that. It was all up to her how much it bothered her that he was younger than she was and that he knew she'd had cancer.

He could hear a different song coming from downstairs.

"Anytime," the guy kept singing.

His sentiment exactly.

Anytime, Meehan. Anytime and anything.

For lack of something better to do, he took a

shower—which he fully expected would turn out to be the high point of his day.

When he came out of the bathroom, he saw a narrow, folded piece of white paper lying on the floor, half of it still under the door.

"Maybe not," he said.

He hobbled over to pick it up. It took a while. His name was written on the outside. He didn't recognize the handwriting. It wasn't Mrs. Bee's. Hers looked just like the row of cursive letters they had had up over the blackboard when he was in grammar school. Even her grocery lists looked like they had been done by the schoolteacher she was.

He unfolded the paper and began to read:

Doyle:
I couldn't get you to the door and I couldn't wait. We've been invited to dinner this evening at seven. I'll be back to get you.

Meehan.

P.S. Refusal is not an option.

Refusal is not an option.
What did that mean?

It sounded like something *he* would say. She should know by now that he wouldn't be refusing anything.

He read the note again, then looked at the clock. He had a little more than an hour to try to figure it out.

Dinner.

No problem. That part he got.

But who would invite the two of them—together—and why? He didn't get it.

Not that it mattered. This was the "anytime" he'd been looking for. He didn't care where they went. The fact that they were making the trip was enough for him.

He took his time shaving. He even put on a little aftershave. Ordinarily, he didn't care for the stuff unless he happened to have a really hot date—and how long had it been since *that* happened? He didn't actually have a hot date now—or at least he didn't think he did. He wasn't quite sure what he had going on here—but whatever it was, he was up for it. Aftershave was definitely in order.

He stood in front of the mirror looking at the final result. He'd had first- and second-degree burns on his face, but there was practically no scarring. His eyes hadn't changed much, in the months since the crash. He and Lieutenant McGraw—and the men in the pictures in Mrs. Bee's World War I book downstairs—all had that same look. It was as if the part of him that had seen Hell itself had crawled up from some dark place and looked out his eyes. He had seen Hell—they all had—and they couldn't tell anybody about it. He couldn't, anyway. He always did a little verbal dance around the army shrink's questions. He was damn good at it, too. Years of practice, thanks to Nina and dear old Mom.

When you forgive yourself.

Meehan's comment suddenly popped into his head. He didn't want to think about that. He wanted to think about dinner and her. How she would look and how she would smell. He was determined to get close enough to find out about the perfume part— was it or wasn't it flowery?—and maybe tonight was the night.

The uniform of the day was the same as always— cargo shorts and a golf shirt. There wasn't much he could do about it. What he had available had to be weighed against what he could tolerate. His mind went immediately to Rita's wedding. He'd done some suffering there. Military uniforms and still-new surgical scars weren't the least bit compatible.

Rita.

He hadn't been thinking about her much of late, but he no longer worried about it. His stomach rumbled. The aromas from the kitchen—meat loaf?— were driving him crazy. Wherever they were going, he hoped the chow was good.

He spent some time policing the apartment— making sure everything was stowed where it should be. There wasn't much straightening up for him to do—he was neat by nature. No, he was neat by the sheer force of his old drill sergeant's will. Even so, if Meehan was actually coming up here, he wanted everything squared away.

He looked at the clock. He still had time to kill.

He should have brought "Michael Mont" and "Fleur" upstairs.

He drank a glass of water, washed the glass and a coffee cup left over from this morning.

Music.

He needed some music to pass the time—except that he already had music. Mrs. Bee's really old old-ies were still coming from downstairs.

He decided not to sit down—which left looking out the window a distinct possibility. After a moment he walked across the room to do just that. Meehan's car was parked in the drive.

Someone knocked. He made an about-face and tried to hurry—but not too much—to answer the door. He didn't want to keep her waiting and he didn't want to seem as eager as he was, either. Meehan didn't scare easy—he knew that—but he didn't want to take any chances.

He took a deep breath and opened the door. There she stood in the hot, stuffy upstairs hallway. It smelled of meat loaf and baking bread and apple pie. And she looked...

Fine.

He looked her over again to be sure, and he saw no evidence that she'd ever been ill. He didn't let himself even consider how extensive her surgery might have been.

She wasn't wearing the opaque dress again. She had on khaki shorts and dark-red T-shirt and sandals. He liked her in shorts. A lot. He liked her in anything.

"Hey," he said. "I got your note."

She didn't say anything.

"What's wrong?" he asked immediately. If this dinner thing had fizzled already, he wanted to know up front.

The big band music from downstairs suddenly stopped.

She looked over her shoulder. "Oh—I'm just a little worried about Mrs. Bee. Are you ready?"

"Roger that," he said.

She stood back so he could come out the door.

"So where are we going?" he asked as he hobbled by her, not quite close enough to identify the scent she was wearing—unless it was meat loaf.

"Downstairs," she said.

"Besides that."

"Downstairs," she said again.

"And that's it?"

"That's it," she said. She started to help him by taking his arm, purely a nurse kind of touch. Even so, she apparently thought better of it and let her hand fall.

"So...we're not going to dinner, then."

"Yes, we are—Mrs. Bee invited us."

Which explains the "refusal is not an option" thing, he thought. He was disappointed that there wasn't a more personal reason for her requiring his presence, but he didn't really mind. He liked Mrs. Bee.

"Cool," he said. "She's been cooking all day."

"She says it's an anniversary."

"Hers and Mr. Bee's?"

"She says no."

"Whose then?"

"I don't know—I was hoping you did."

"Nope. So how is Scottie?"

She stopped walking, and so did he. He didn't think she was going to answer.

"He's…worried about his mother," she said after some consideration.

"Yeah, he would be, wouldn't he?"

"Did he say something to you?"

"Not exactly. He knew she was crying about something and he pretty much understood that he had to stay out of the way. He's a good little kid."

Meehan was staring at him in that way she had. "Yes. He is."

She started walking again, and he went with her.

"You know you're getting around a lot better?" she said as he tackled the stairs.

"Am I?" he asked, because "better" or not, it still hurt.

"Damn straight," she said, and he grinned.

Mrs. Bee was standing at the bottom of the stairs, and she'd shown up "battle rattle"—ready for anything. She was all dressed up—beauty parlor, makeup, jewelry, the works. Maybe even a new dress.

"Don't mention the magazine," he said to Meehan under his breath.

"Why?"

"Because," he said, trying not to move his lips.

"You look nice, Mrs. Bee," he said on the way down, because she did and because his grandmother had always told him women appreciated a sincere compliment—whereas an insincere one could get him hurt.

"Thank you, Calvin. I'm so glad you and Katie could come tonight."

"Smells good, Mrs. Bee. Special occasion, huh?"

"It is to me, Calvin—and one I can't share with just anybody. I haven't been keeping my word about remembering, these last few years. This year I'm making up for it. Come into the dining room. Everything is ready. Ordinarily we'd chat for a while in the front parlor, but I'm a little tired. I hope you're hungry, Katie. Calvin, I *know* you are."

"You got my number, Mrs. Bee," he said, following her and Meehan. Everything was indeed ready. The table was set in what must be her best china. The food was already on the table—meat loaf, as he already suspected, mashed potatoes and gravy, cole slaw, deviled eggs, huge homemade rolls, green beans with white corn, a big pitcher of iced tea with lemons floating on top, two pies—one with icing.

French apple, he guessed.

And there were flowers—roses and something or other and white candles that had already been lit. The table looked like a page out of a magazine.

"The menu is nothing fancy," Mrs. Bee said. "He asked me to fix all his favorites for him when he came home—but of course, he didn't."

Doyle exchanged a look with Meehan. He was on the verge of asking who "he" was, but he decided to restrain his "hunt the hill" mind-set again, at least for the moment. Mrs. Bee patted the back of a dining room chair as she went around the table.

"You sit here, Calvin—and, Katie, you over there."

"The table is beautiful," Meehan said as she took her seat.

"Yes, if I do say so myself," Mrs. Bee said. "I promised, you see."

Doyle didn't see, and he didn't think Meehan did—but neither of them said so. He suddenly realized that the table was set for four. As soon as he and Meehan were seated, Mrs. Bee reached for their hands and said a prayer that included a petition for his and Meehan's well-being.

"Comfort food," she said as soon as she was done, handing Doyle the huge bowl of mashed potatoes. Then, "Oh, I forgot the music."

"I'll get it, Mrs. Bee," Meehan said.

"Oh, good," she said. "I'm still a little scared of that new machine. It does things with those little silver records all by itself. I told that grandson of mine I didn't need it, but he insisted.''

When Meehan got up from the table, Doyle watched her walk to the new stereo in the parlor just off the dining room door, intent on verifying one more time that she was as good-looking as he'd only just noticed.

Yes and yes. She was good-looking in both directions.

When Meehan sat down again, he glanced at Mrs. Bee—and realized that she hadn't missed his interest in her other guest. She was a sharp old lady. Nothing got by her.

The music started almost immediately. He wondered idly if the grandson had given Mrs. Bee a big band CD or if she'd bought it herself. A CD ought to be a piece of cake for anyone as adventurous in her purchases as she was. He could just see her in the mall music store.

In a moment Frank Sinatra began to sing something that had to be called ''Don't Forget Tonight Tomorrow.''

Doyle could see that the song brought back memories. He thought for a moment Mrs. Bee was going to cry, and he plunged into a conversation to get her mind off it. He told her about living on Pop Doyle's farm and his rule for a happy life.

''Plow straight, plant well, cultivate carefully and harvest like you mean it. If you always do that, he said, whatever bad happens ain't your fault.''

Then he told her about his grandmother Doyle and how much she loved to cook. Then he switched to her garden and how she spent hours "putting up" the tomatoes and corn, white cucumbers, and the green beans she grew every summer. She even canned sausage, he told her—and always in a blue Mason jar.

"Did you help?" Meehan asked when she could get a word in.

"Had to," he said. "I couldn't outrun her."

Mrs. Bee finally managed a smile and passed another bowl. Frank Sinatra gave way to somebody singing happily about a tomato and Plato, baloney and Tony.

They don't make songs like they used to, Doyle thought. The meal continued, and the conversation flourished without his help. Meehan held up her end with comments on the possibility of afternoon and evening thundershowers, her job at the post hospital and world headlines. She didn't go anywhere near the girlie magazine.

They didn't make cooks like they used to, either, and most of the time he was only half listening. Everything tasted so good. At one point he looked up from his enjoyment to find both women watching him. He winked at Mrs. Bee, making her smile, and no one mentioned the empty chair.

The wind had picked up outside. There was a rumble of thunder, and the candles flickered in the cross breeze from the open windows. The first drops of rain were beginning to fall by the time Mrs. Bee was ready to cut the apple pie. The phone rang—once.

"Someone dialed before they remembered," Mrs. Bee said. "Lula Mae and the girls know not to call me today."

"Why is that, Mrs. Bee?" he asked, because he thought it was time.

"He was a soldier—a paratrooper," she said instead of answering. "Like you, Calvin."

"I didn't know Mr. Bee was a paratrooper," Meehan said.

"No. Not Mr. Bee."

The old lady gave a quiet sigh and looked past him toward the empty chair. "He was so good-looking." She suddenly smiled. "But so was I—that boy didn't stand a chance."

"You're still good-looking, Mrs. Bee," Doyle said, and she laughed out loud.

"And soldiers never change, do they, Katie?"

"Never," Meehan assured her.

"His name was William Gaffney," Mrs. Bee said wistfully. "Everybody called him 'Bud.' I met him on a bus from Savannah to Fayetteville—my fiancé was stationed at Fort Bragg—that wasn't Mr. Bee, either," she added mischievously. "*His* name was Jeffrey McCall."

Any kin to Pitty-Pat? Doyle almost asked.

"I was going to see him," Mrs. Bee said. "His sister was supposed to chaperon, but she was in the back of the bus. She was kind of fast,'' Mrs. Bee said, lowering her voice, as if she didn't want just anybody to hear her.

Kin to Pitty-Pat, he decided.

''I think Bud might have thought I was fast, too—at first—since I was traveling with her. But I wasn't. I was just young...and bewildered. Everything was happening so fast—the war, all the boys leaving. Boys I'd known all my life. All of us young girls knew there was a good chance we'd never see them again. Everybody was crazy to get married, and here I was engaged when I didn't really know how in this world I had gotten to that point. I'd known Jeffrey for ages—since we were children—and then there he was in uniform, looking so handsome and not quite able to hide how scared he was, and he asked me. I must have said yes—but to this day, I don't remember doing it. I don't think I realized how serious it all was until my mother said I could go to Fort Bragg to see him without her.

''I remember being on that bus, though. It stopped at nearly every wide place in the road. It was so hot, and the bus was packed. Every time it stopped, I'd think they couldn't possibly get one more person on, but they always did somehow. The woman I was sitting next to was wearing Blue Waltz perfume—the kind you could buy at the dime store. It was so *strong*. I was sitting by a window, but I couldn't get it open, and I was getting sicker and sicker. We finally stopped at this little service station in the middle of nowhere. It had a really steep roof.'' She held up her hands to show them how steep. ''And big shade trees with the trunks whitewashed—they don't do that much nowadays—and some picnic tables. It was a kind of place where they'd let everybody get off and get something to drink and take the children to the rest room. I was feeling so bad, and he got me a bottle of cola. He'd been watching me, you see, and he knew I wasn't feeling well. The drink was all icy. The best cola I ever had. I wanted to pay him for it, but he wouldn't let me.

''Well, it made me feel better, and we talked all the way to Fayetteville, both of us standing up because I'd lost my seat and there weren't any more— and me in high heels, too. Brown-and-white spectator pumps. You didn't go anywhere in public in those days unless you had on high heels. And you didn't go bare-legged, either. I had on my mother's last pair of silk stockings. They were too small because the toes had been darned so many times, and between the stockings and the heels and the heat— and being totally mortified by what Jeffrey's sister was doing in the back of the bus—I'd never been so miserable in my whole life. Or so happy. I just knew in my heart something marvelous was happening.'' She reached for the tea pitcher and refilled Meehan's glass.

''Well, I broke my engagement that weekend,'' she continued. ''It was a hard thing to do. Both our mothers cried for days. I wasn't sure I'd ever see

Bud again, but I was very sure I didn't want to marry Jeffrey just because there was a war on and I felt sorry for him. I'd given Bud my name and address, and I watched for the mailman every day after that, as if it was a matter of life and death— and I guess maybe it was. He wrote me a letter— he was very good at writing letters. Some people have that knack, you know. When you read them, it's as if they're actually speaking to you. I'd been waiting for days and days, praying he would write to me—and then when the letter finally came, when I finally saw it there in the mailbox, I didn't open it. Not at first. I just held it and looked at it. I wanted to make the feeling last, you see. That wonderful feeling of expectation that comes when you think something good is about to happen and your life is going to change forever.

"He came to Savannah to see me—when he could only stay a couple of hours. After that, he hitchhiked down there every chance he got—he used to take me to this Irish pub down on the riverfront. I wasn't old enough to be in there—my mother would have had a fit if she'd known—but most places didn't bother too much about that kind of thing, because of the war and so many boys going overseas all the time. We went for the music, believe it or not. It was a lot like your uncle Patrick's place, Katie—the customers could sing something for the crowd if they wanted to. The last time we went there, Bud went up to the microphone. I thought it would be something funny—because he was so funny—and maybe a little risqué, but it wasn't. He sang this sad song about a soldier looking for the one he could love and finally finding her. There was a part in it about him praying for angels to always protect her—it was so beautiful and it was for me. There weren't many dry eyes in the pub that night, I can tell you.''

"Did you marry him, Mrs. Bee?" Meehan asked, handing Doyle the second piece of pie she'd cut for him.

"He asked me. And I got all silly about it. I wanted him to be my husband more than I'd ever wanted anything in this world, but I told him no because I still regretted the brainless way I'd gotten engaged to Jeffrey. I said something about us not knowing if what we felt was real and that only time would tell.

"He said time was something we might never have—and even if we did, there were no guarantees. Our chance had come along when the whole world was in a mess, he said, so we had to make do— because if we didn't, maybe we'd would lose something really precious, something other people only dream about.

"I'm happy to say I didn't stay silly for long. We eloped," she said with a slight smile. "I met him about halfway—in a little county seat in South Carolina. It was a real leap of faith for me. I kept thinking he wouldn't come—he'd have a change of heart or maybe he'd get sent overseas and I'd never see him again and never know what happened to him. He was late, but we made it—just barely. He was sent to the West Coast right after that. I think the government did that to fool the German spies. They sent them west—when they were really going to Europe. Anyway, he went overseas. He was killed in the Normandy invasion—it was a very bad place for paratroopers. He's buried in the cemetery there. The news about him came in the middle of *Fibber McGee and Molly.* That's a radio program. I was at home with my mother and sisters, and we were all laughing. Somehow you just never think you could get such bad news in the middle of something like *Fibber McGee and Molly*—oh, now I've made you both uncomfortable. I didn't want to do that. It's just that I promised him I'd make him his favorite dinner when he came home again. He didn't come home, but I still make the dinner sometimes—on our anniversary. It's my way of remembering him. I haven't done it in a long time—but this year I felt that I really wanted to. He would have liked the two of you so much. Mr. Bee and I had a good life together—but I haven't forgotten Bud. Someone has to remember, you see. He didn't have any family but me.''

Mrs. Bee slowly slid back her chair. ''You know, I'm much more tired than I thought. I missed my nap this afternoon, and I think I'll just wish the two of you good-night and go on to bed now. Thank you both.''

"Thank *you*, Mrs. Bee," Doyle said. "I've never had a better meal anywhere."

"I'm glad, Calvin. Oh, the leftovers—"

"We'll put the leftovers away," Meehan said.

"All right. If you're sure you don't mind. I do hate to see food go to waste—but leave the dishes. I'll see to those tomorrow."

Meehan got up with Mrs. Bee, making sure she had her hand there just when Mrs. Bee needed it and walking with her to the back of the house. Doyle sat looking at the table. It was still raining, but gently now, a steady pattering he could hear along the edge of the porch. After a moment, he got to his feet and extinguished the candles. He'd been sitting too long. He'd gotten lost in the good eating and in Mrs. Bee's sad story of Bud Gaffney—or, more accurately, in Meehan's reaction to it. It had affected her, just as it had him, maybe because it was Mrs. Bee who was telling it.

Meehan came back. She immediately began to gather up bowls and take them into the kitchen. He carried what he could and followed along after her, neither of them talking as they began the cleanup.

He ran hot water into the sink and squirted in some dish detergent while she scraped plates and brought them to him. At one point his arm brushed hers. He felt it deep, but if she even noticed, it didn't show—except that she left the room immediately and headed back to the dining room. In a moment the big band music started again, an orchestra playing something with...

What did they call it back then? Bounce? Jump?

It didn't really matter. This was Bud Gaffney's party; whatever it was was altogether appropriate.

Meehan returned carrying a few stray spoons and a glass. She put them on the counter next to the sink. Carefully. So she wouldn't touch him again.

"I'll do that," she said of the dish washing.

"No, it's okay. I can do it," he said.

"Will you sit down? You're hurting. You can dry."

He was hurting, but he hesitated. Old habits died hard, regardless of what he'd said earlier about feeling free to give in to the pain in her presence.

After a moment he dried his hands and moved one of the kitchen chairs closer and sat down. She handed him a dish towel to use, but they didn't talk. They simply worked on getting the kitchen squared away. Mrs. Bee was one of those cooks who washed the pans as soon as she put the food into the bowls, so it wouldn't take long.

"How's your other charity case?" he asked at one point, and he realized the minute he said it that her guard went up, he supposed because she thought that he was making some extremely obscure reference to her former boyfriend.

"Coyote Jane," he said. "White fur. Low to the ground."

"She's fine. What did you mean 'other' charity case."

"I meant me—I thought maybe you had something to do with my getting a Chain of Concern person."

"I did," she said, glancing at him. "You've got too much time on your hands."

"Well, you've got me there," he said. He picked up another wet plate and began to dry it. "How mad do you think Mrs. Bee is going to be?" he asked to keep the conversation going. "Because you washed the dishes."

"She's not going to be mad at *me,*" Meehan said. "I'm going to tell her *you* did it."

He laughed. "Oh, thanks. She'll believe you, too."

The conversation immediately lagged, and he never was one to leave well enough alone.

"So, have you ever been married?" he asked.

"Yes," she said without looking at him.

Yes.

He didn't see how she couldn't have been at some point—she was pretty and smart—but he still wasn't all that happy to hear it.

"What happened?"

"He divorced me."

"What, is he crazy?" he said in all seriousness. He finished drying a dinner plate, and when he looked up, she had stopped washing dishes.

"One of us was," she said after a moment.

"What happened?"

"Nothing much," she said, putting the silverware into the sink, and for once, he didn't sense her internal struggle not to answer him. "I met him when I was in nursing school—he was a med student—a good one. We got married right after I graduated. We eloped—he said it would be better if his family heard about the marriage after the fact. It wasn't better. His father was very upset and threatened all kinds of financial repercussions. But he said his family would get used to the idea, and he asked me to come back here and wait while he got it all straightened out. I didn't have a job yet, so I did. While I was waiting, I was served with divorce papers—sued for divorce on the grounds of abandonment. And that, as they say, was that."

Doyle didn't say anything, and she went back to washing spoons and forks. They finished the rest of the dishes in silence.

He handed her the dish towel and got to his feet. "Meehan—"

"I'm going to check the dining room," she said, stepping around him.

He thought that she'd already done that, but he didn't say so. He followed her as far as the dim hallway and stood waiting for her to come back. She wasn't gone long. The big band music changed to something slow and sad by the time she walked into the hallway again. She obviously didn't expect to see him there.

"So," he said. "You want to dance?"

"Sure. Who with?"

"*Me*. Are you trying to hurt my feelings here or what?"

"Oh, sorry. When I think of dancing, somehow you don't automatically spring to mind."

"I can dance. This kind of dancing anyway. Let me show you…"

He propped his cane against the wall, then took her by the hand and had her in dance position before she could protest. She wasn't exactly relaxed, but she wasn't exactly resisting. He was encouraged enough to go on with it.

A cool, rain-driven breeze came in through the front screen door, making the hallway perfect for this kind of thing—whatever this kind of thing might be.

The melancholy music swirled around them.

"I'll Be Seeing You."

The song sounded as if the recording had been done in a stairwell, and the echo quality made it seem even more lonely. He was getting the emotion behind it loud and clear. The guy was gone; the girl singer was miserable, in the same way Mrs. Bee must have been miserable.

Meehan's hand relaxed in his. He couldn't believe she was putting up with this. He got a whiff of the perfume she wore. He couldn't identify it exactly; maybe it was some kind of flowers, maybe not.

But she smelled so good! Her hair, her skin. He

didn't dare bring her any closer, but, man, he wanted to. He wanted her head on his shoulder. He wanted to feel her body pressed against his. He swayed her gently to the music. Every now and then he even moved his feet. People passing on the street could probably see them. He wondered if Mrs. Bee and Bud Gaffney had ever danced like this. Incredible. After all this time she still missed the guy.

"She's so sad tonight," Meehan said, as if she had been thinking of Mrs. Bee, too.

"Yeah. But it's not what you think. It's just a scar."

"Just a scar. I don't know what that means."

"It means scars can hurt sometimes—if you hit them hard enough—but they're not the wound. That's healed."

"Are we talking about your surgery or Rita?"

"Both," he said easily. "And maybe your ex-husband. I care about Rita. I always will. If she ever came to me for help, I'd help her. But she's a scar, just like the scars on my legs. Scars don't keep me from dancing—if I try hard enough—or you, either. See?"

She didn't answer him; she looked up at him. Even in the dim light he could see her beautiful eyes. The song ended, but he didn't immediately let her go.

She was still looking at him. He could kiss her now, he thought. He could kiss her, and she'd let him do it.

He leaned down. His hand slid to the center of her back.

Kate.

"Kate?" someone said at the screen door, and she immediately stepped away. He looked around to see. It was the sister—Scottie's mother.

"Kate," the sister said again. "I didn't mean—I'm sorry."

"I have to go," Meehan said, slipping past him. She walked quickly to the screen door, but she looked back at him once before she disappeared into the rainy summer night.

Chapter Seven

Now what?

He didn't sleep much. His legs hurt, and he kept thinking about Meehan.

Kate.

Not Katherine. Not Katie.

Kate.

The woman who was getting to him regardless of the fact that it was all wrong, and it was about as mismatched as it could get, and it was the kind of deal that could end up with good old Bugs Doyle getting left in the proverbial dirt.

But he was nothing if not a realist, and there was something going on here. He felt it every time he looked into her eyes, every time he got within ten feet of her. He had felt it when they danced. He could still feel it. He was willing to admit that when it came to women, he had had more than one occasion of being terminally dense—but this wasn't one of them. He was *not* wrong about it. Which brought him back to his original question.

Now what?

Mrs. Bee seemed to be her usual chipper self today. She'd gone someplace several times in Thelma and Louise, and she'd even had the energy to get after him for ignoring her orders about leaving the dirty dishes. Even so, he made a point of hanging around downstairs in the Bee Library. Mrs. Bee came through a time or two—she even stopped to chat, but she made no mention of Meehan. He had no idea what kind of work schedule Meehan was on now, but it was clear to him that he was just going to have to "hunt the hill," and that's all there was to it.

"Mrs. Bee, have you seen Meehan today?" he asked when she was dusting the little china dogs on the mantel.

"Oh, yes," Mrs. Bee said without missing a dog. But that was all she said.

"You've…known her a long time, I guess."

"A long time," she agreed, still dusting. "That was her parents' house next door. Mr. Bee and I were living here when the family moved in. There were four girls. Let's see now. Katie and Arley— Arley's the youngest. And Gwen—she's older than they are. And Grace—she's the oldest. Katie is the one who looks after everybody. Grace is the bossy one. Gwen is the timid one. Arley is the handful."

"Which one belongs to Scottie?"

"Arley."

Figures, Doyle thought, his earlier, "poor old Scottie" opinion now reaffirmed.

"What about Meehan's ex-husband?" he asked, getting to the point of the conversation. "Did you know him?"

"Oh, my, no," Mrs. Bee said. "I don't think I would have wanted to. Katie doesn't talk about him to anyone, and I would never ask."

Unlike some people he could name.

A car horn honked in the driveway.

"That's Lula Mae," Mrs. Bee said. "I'll be at the church until I don't know when. If you leave, will you lock the house, Calvin?"

"Sure thing, Mrs. Bee."

"And, Calvin?"

"Yeah, Mrs. Bee?"

He waited for her to say something—she obviously wanted to—but she sighed instead.

"You're a good boy, Calvin," she said, hurrying away.

He stood for a moment, thinking.

Meehan didn't talk about the ex-husband to anyone—but she'd told him. Of course, he'd asked about it, but she didn't have to oblige. And she'd danced with him. She might have even done more if the sister—Arley—hadn't crashed the party. There had to be a next logical step to take here—only he had no idea what it was.

He decided to go outside to see if Meehan was right, if nothing else. Maybe he was getting around better.

Mrs. Bee hadn't put Thelma and Louise back into the shed after her final run. The vintage car sat in the driveway, mud-spattered from last night's rain. He stood on the porch for a moment, then went back inside and into the kitchen. It didn't take him long to locate Mrs. Bee's all-purpose enamel bucket and some clean rags in the pantry. The least he could do was spiff up her car a little. It would give him something to do to pass the time—right where he could see Meehan if she came back.

It took him a while to get the garden hose out of the tomato patch and dragged to the car, but he managed eventually. The car was mostly in the shade, which was a good thing. It was hot outside. Somebody close by was playing the radio—a country-western station, which suited him just fine.

He worked slowly and methodically at rinsing the mud off the fenders, trying to keep his mind on the job and not on anything else, singing along with the radio whenever anything caught his fancy. At one point he took off his T-shirt—and heard a small gasp.

He looked around. Three women stood at the edge of Meehan's backyard—huddled together—staring.

He had the sudden sense that the only thing missing was the cauldron. He'd never seen such an array of facial expressions—one annoyed, one worried and one very appreciative of his buff bare chest.

He didn't see any cars in the drive—he could only assume that they had either arrived by broom or they had parked on the street. And, big sunglasses or not, he recognized one of them—the handful, Arley.

The women immediately got busy looking busy. He nodded in their direction, but he didn't say anything, and neither did they. He went back to washing Mrs. Bee's car.

Apparently, women, no matter what age they were, had no idea how well a man could hear—when he wanted to.

"Is that him?" one of them whispered.

"Yes," someone—Arley—answered.

"Are you sure?"

"Yes, I'm sure. I've seen him more than once, you know."

"How old do you think he is?"

"Well, how should I know? I didn't ask him—and I sure didn't ask Kate."

"What happened to him?"

"Helicopter crash, *she* said."

"Are you sure he and Kate were—"

"I'm sure!"

"We shouldn't be doing this," another voice said. "This is none of our business. We should *not* be doing this—"

"Excuse me!" the first voice called loudly, and he looked around.

"Hi," she said. "You're Kate's friend, right?" she asked, but she didn't give him a chance to answer. "She's having a little...get-together—steaks on the grill kind of thing—this evening. Can you come?"

Slick, he thought. He knew damn well she was making it up as she went along, but she got the invitation out and never once did she say it was Meehan's idea. He strongly suspected that Meehan didn't have a clue that she was entertaining this evening.

"Sure," he said, anyway. "What time?" He wanted to go so he could see what she was going to do to them, if nothing else.

"Six o'clock. Sharp," the sister who had to be Grace, the bossy one, said.

"Okay," he said. "Want me to bring anything?"

"Just yourself."

"I can handle that," he said, and she forced a smile. He went back to washing the car.

"Kate is going to kill you, you know that," he heard the sister who must be timid Gwen say.

"Will you stop worrying? If she won't tell us what's going on, it falls on us to find out the best way we can."

"Yes, well, I hope you like the color green—because she's going to turn all three of us into frogs."

Doyle laughed softly to himself. This was going to be so good. Or bad. Clearly, the sisters thought they had cause for alarm where he and Meehan were concerned, and he couldn't help but feel encouraged. Maybe it was more than just Arley seeing them *not* dancing. Maybe Meehan had said something—protested too much.

He kept working on Mrs. Bee's car, feeling the eyes on him from the row of windows at the back of Meehan's house. He was good at that—feeling eyes—thanks to all his peacekeeping deployments to places that were anything but peaceful. Coyote Jane was probably looking out the window, too.

He was tired when he finished, from the unaccustomed exertion and from the lack of sleep. He went inside and showered, then opted for a short nap under the heated throw before he went to the impromptu get-together next door. He was looking forward to seeing Meehan—if she didn't find out what her sisters had planned and make a run for it.

He woke up to a soft knock on the door. He had been sleeping so soundly it took him a moment to orient himself.

"In," he said when the knock sounded again. He had been reasonably comfortable with the throw over his legs, and he was in no hurry to make things hurt. He expected to see Mrs. Bee, but Meehan stepped through the doorway.

"I understand I've been stood up," she said.

With considerable effort he sat on the side of the bed. "Stood up?"

"The steaks are on the grill and no Doyle. I'm willing to accept that you might stand *me* up, but you wouldn't miss a steak—so I figured I'd come and see—especially after I heard you'd been washing cars. So. How bad are your legs hurting?"

"Not bad," he said.

"You are such a liar," she said in exasperation, and he couldn't keep from smiling.

"Okay. Bad. For a while. They're pretty good at the moment, though."

"So are you up for the inquisition?"

"Are you?"

"No—I feel like an idiot. I'm too old for this—but I guess I need your help. If you can come over and make an appearance—just long enough to show them there is absolutely nothing going on between you and me, I'd appreciate it. You'll get a steak out of it, and I'll get some peace and quiet. Okay?"

He was looking at her, thinking how pretty she looked and about taking the pins out of her hair and letting it fall down. There was no denying it. Her pants were by no means as safe as he'd led her to believe.

"Doyle?" she prompted.

"Lead the way," he said. "But not too fast."

"You understand the plan," she said as he unplugged the throw and got up from the bed.

"Affirmative. There is absolutely nothing between us."

"And you'll convince my sisters."

"How am I going to do that?"

"Just be...normal. You know...indifferent."

Of all the things he might have been in her presence lately, "indifferent" wasn't one of them, but he didn't say so.

"Wouldn't it be easier if I just stayed here? And they think I really did stand you up?"

"No," she said pointedly. "Your not showing up would just put blood in the water. My sisters travel in a pack, and they think I'm getting into something with the potential for a lot of trouble and heartache. Believe me, they never give up."

"Can't you just rip them a new one?"

"That's Plan B—I promised our mother I'd do what I could to keep the peace."

"Got your work cut out for you, huh?" he said.

She ignored his remark. "Plan A is simply letting them see us together. Then they can see for themselves that I'm not trying to hide anything, and they'll go run somebody else's life."

"Works for me," he said.

"Good."

"I get the steak either way, though," he said, and she grinned.

"Deal," she said.

"Should I apologize?" she asked as they crossed the yard.

"For what?"

"For whatever my sisters said to you. I realize they can be less than subtle."

"Nobody said anything worth an apology," he said, resting for a moment before he tried walking again.

She gave a sharp sigh. "I can't believe I'm doing this. You're one of my *patients,* and I'm dragging you over here when you should be resting."

"I'm not a patient, I'm a friend. And I can rest anywhere. So do they have husbands—the sisters?"

"Yes."

"Where are they?"

"Hiding if they know what's good for them."

He got a whiff of the steaks on the charcoal grill. "Man, that smells good."

Good enough to entice him into walking again.

"You look nice," he said as he hobbled along. "What?" he added, because of her extremely incredulous look.

"You can't say things like that!" she whispered. "I told you, they think something is going on!"

"Well, did they hear me? No. I don't think it would matter if they did."

"And I don't think you understand this situation."

"Sure I do. What's not to understand? Your sisters travel in a pack, and they think you're doing the dirty-dirty with me. You don't want them to, and they're not about to butt out, so you're going to implement Plan A—when you'd really rather lock and load. Unfortunately, your mama put it on your shoulders to keep the peace and you don't feel like you can tell them where to park it no matter how bad you want to, so you're stuck with making nice. My personal opinion is that what you need here is a good slash-and-burn policy, so that you can put an end to this kind of meddling once and for all—but, what do I know? I couldn't handle my female relatives, either. This is your operation all the way, and I got it. No problem.''

She looked at him doubtfully.

''I got it, I got it,'' he assured her.

She sighed again. Clearly, she really was bothered about all this.

All three sisters were on the alert and waiting for him to reach the patio.

''You've met my sisters,'' Meehan said when they were close enough, holding out a hand in their direction.

''Not exactly,'' he answered truthfully.

''Well, this is Grace,'' she said, indicating the tall one he had already guessed was the bossy one. ''This is Gwen and Arley. And Scottie you know.''

He hadn't realized the kid was on the premises. ''Hey, buddy. How's it going? You got any more rocks?''

To his surprise the boy ran to him, nearly bowling him over with an enthusiastic hug to the knees.

''This is Bugs,'' Scottie told his aunts. ''He

doesn't wait for the plane to land—come on, come on, Bugs!'' he said, pulling Doyle by his free hand. ''Come and see!''

Doyle let himself be taken into the house to the same couch he'd spent the night on, and he immediately made a mental note not to say anything about *that*.

In any event, it seemed as good a place as any for him to be ''indifferent.'' The couch was in the traffic pattern from the patio to the kitchen. The sisters walked back and forth, all three of them keeping their sights on him as if they thought he might make off with the silverware. He was not in what he would call a target-rich environment. There was only one. Him.

Scottie didn't have his rocks with him this time; he had books. A *lot* of books. Doyle ended up sitting with a cat under one arm and a boy under the other, and the entire stack of books on his lap. Meehan brought him a footstool, and Grace brought him a glass of iced tea. Arley frowned—and Gwen cut her finger on something lethal in the kitchen.

He read. And read. By the third book, two-thirds of the couch potatoes were fast asleep.

''I'll take those,'' Meehan said, lifting the books off his knees. ''And that,'' she said of Scottie.

''He's all right. I don't mind.''

''I'll just move him to the other end so he can stretch out. The steaks are almost ready.''

''Great,'' he said, taking advantage of the opportunity to watch her while she put Scottie into a more restful position on the couch. The boy didn't wake.

"Big day, I guess," Doyle said, nodding in Scottie's direction.

"Are you all right?" Meehan asked.

"Who me? I'm fine. Why?"

"I thought maybe you had a big day, too."

"I washed a car. Period."

"I didn't know you were going to have to baby-sit again."

He looked into her eyes, just to see if she'd let him. She did—briefly.

"He's not any trouble."

"I wish his father felt that way," she said.

"So where is his father?" he asked. Scottie wasn't the first little kid he'd seen starved for male attention.

"With his new girlfriend."

"We have a problem, Kate," Grace called from the patio.

"There's my cue," she said wearily. "It can't be Gwen—she's run out of fingers."

"Are you getting the third degree out there?" he asked.

"You bet," she assured him. She walked off to see what Grace wanted, and Arley almost immediately took her place. She sat down on the coffee table and looked at him a long time before she said anything. He had thought the first time he saw her that she looked like a younger version of Meehan.

He still did. There was something missing in the eyes, though. A lot of something missing.

"So," she said finally. "Is it serious?"

"Is what serious?" he asked, deciding to make The Handful work at it.

"This thing between you and Kate," she said.

"It's not serious," he said. *Yet.*

"That's not what she says."

"No?"

"You know, you're really not her type," she said, completely changing directions.

"Correct," he said, because she'd definitely gotten that right. He'd been all over the world, and about all he had to show for it was a bunch of chewing gum stickers—pictures of naked women that came in nickel packs of chewing gum the Balkan locals sold to peacekeeping soldiers to help make ends meet. It would be a *long* time before he'd be running around with a bag of gourmet bagels and driving an expensive silver car. If ever.

The cat got up and immediately lay down again, its head now resting conveniently under his fingers. He gave it a token scratch between the ears and once again he could feel it purring.

"Are you the reason she dumped Paul?" Arley asked, he thought, more to see if she could get to him than because she actually wanted to know.

"Don't think so. I don't even know who Paul is."

"Well, he was the love of her life until a couple of weeks ago."

"Oh, you mean the real estate guy. No. I'm not the reason."

"I don't believe you," she said.

"Yeah, well, I can't help that. So what about you?"

"Me?"

"Yeah. What about this guy you think you love with all your heart."

Her eyes flashed—and for a moment he thought she was going to hit him with something.

"*That* is none of your business."

He smiled. "Oh, I see. Dishing it out is your thing."

She got up from the coffee table and left. Grace almost immediately took up the slack. Grace didn't look like Meehan. At all. She had the same air of competence, but that was about it. This woman was born to command. She couldn't be bothered with lipstick or shaving her legs, and Calvin "Bugs" Doyle had her full attention.

"Has everybody abandoned you?" she asked. She sat in the nearest chair.

"No, I'm fine," he said. "How's Gwen doing?"

"Oh, she's gotten a new wound. Some people have no business around sharp objects. So. You're Kate's friend."

"Yes," he answered truthfully.

"And?"

"And...whatever else I am is none of your business," he said easily. "To tell you the truth, I'm a little surprised you think so."

"She's my sister. And she hasn't had the best judgment when it comes to men."

"People usually believe what the people they love tell them—until they have good reason not to, don't you think? It's got nothing to do with judgment."

"You have a very simplistic way of looking at a very complicated situation," she said.

"Meaning?"

"Meaning Kate has…baggage. Things someone like you wouldn't want to have to deal with."

"Someone like me? I know about the ex-husband, Grace. I know about the real estate guy. And I know about the cancer," he said.

She stared at him, clearly surprised that she didn't have the upper hand here. He didn't think she was used to it, and he was definitely sure she didn't like it.

"You don't have to worry," he said after a moment. "You and Gwen and Arley have got the cart way before the horse. Right now Kate's a friend. Period. But whichever way it goes, I don't think you're going to have much to say about it."

Scottie stirred on the couch and turned over. Gwen burst through the door carrying a platter of steaks that was clearly too hot to handle.

"Too many mosquitoes to eat outside!" she said on the run. "Come on, everybody!"

Grace got up from the chair and followed her into

the kitchen. Doyle stayed where he was, waiting for
Arley to get by and Meehan to show. She didn't. He
got up from the couch, trying not to jiggle Scottie
any more than he could help, and walked to the
door. Meehan was sitting on top of the wooden table
she used when she repotted her flowers.

He opened the door and went out. She looked
around when she heard him, but she didn't say anything.

"So how's it going?" he asked when he was
close enough.

"I can't find any cigarettes," she said. She picked
up something—sunflower seeds—off the table and
leaned over to toss them nearer the bird feeders.

"Can't help you. Don't smoke."

"Me, either," she said, and they both laughed.

"That bad, huh?"

"Yeah," she said, sighing. "Arley and I had
words—right after Grace and I had words."

"How about Gwen? Was she in there anywhere?"

"No—but the whole business made her cry."

They both looked up at the moonlit sky. He could
hear crickets and tree frogs. It was a beautiful summer night.

"I need to ask you something," he said after a
moment. "It's serious."

"I don't think I'm up to anything 'serious.'"

"It's about you and me."

"There is no you and me. Bugs, what you're feeling—or think you're feeling—has to do with you

being hurt so badly and being a patient on my ward. It's a very common occurrence.''

''You mean I like you as much as I do because you helped me when I really needed it.''

''Exactly.''

''Is that a two-way thing?'' he asked.

''I don't know what you mean.''

''I mean who got who in out of the rain? Does that count as me helping you when *you* really needed it? Is this helping business a two-way thing or not?''

She didn't say anything, and he took a step closer.

''You're on the rebound,'' she said.

''So are you, and don't try to stonewall me. I still want to ask you something,'' he said, stopping just short of her knees. He leaned his cane against the table and reached out and took her left hand and placed it firmly against his shoulder.

He held up one finger in warning when she was about to pull it away. ''Just cut me a little slack, okay?''

Then he took the other one and placed it on his other shoulder.

''Doyle, what are you doing…?''

''I'm making sure you know that you're the one in control here. You might as well let me ask what I want to ask and get it over with,'' he said. ''You never can tell. Slash-and-burn might work with me, too. I'm about to give you a great opportunity to do it.''

She sighed. "All right. Ask."

But he didn't ask. He looked into her eyes, and she looked back.

Kate, he thought. Kate...

"Are you going to let me kiss you?" he asked quietly.

It was the absolute last thing she expected. Her fingers tightened on his shoulders, but she didn't push him away. He could hear the sisters banging pots and sliding chairs in the kitchen.

"Arc you?" he asked again, leaning closer. Her knees pressed into his belly, his hands rested on the table on either side of her thighs. He had her surrounded, trapped, but he was still asking.

"Are you?" he said a third time, bypassing her mouth to whisper in her ear.

He waited. It took every ounce of control he had to do it. She smelled so good, and the taste of her was already in his mind. Her fingers dug into his shoulders, but she still didn't push him away.

"Kate," he whispered, and she made a small, needy sound that tore his heart out.

She leaned forward. Her arms slid around him, and she rested her head on his shoulder for a moment, clinging to him before she turned her head and pressed her mouth against his. The kiss was hard and deep and...

He couldn't get enough of her, couldn't get her close enough. He was starving.

Starving...

But he was the one who broke away. He stood there, hands shaking, ready to go off. He had never felt anything so intense. Never. It wasn't because he'd been so long without. And this wasn't one of those love-the-one-you're-with, heavy-breathing sessions. He'd had enough of those to know.

He could feel eyes watching from the windows again.

"This is either the beginning or the end," he said. "You know that, don't you?"

But he didn't wait for her to answer. He picked up his cane and, with what little willpower he had remaining, he walked to the edge of the patio and down the steps toward Mrs. Bee's.

Chapter Eight

Kate.

The last thing on his mind when he finally fell asleep and the first thing on his mind this morning—besides the knocking on the door.

He forced himself out of bed and made his way to answer it, hoping.

Hoping...

"Okay, hoss, let's ride," the soldier in the hallway said when he opened the door.

Doyle stood staring at him, noting the lesser rank and searching for some clue as to his purpose. Absolutely nothing came to mind.

"What?" he said pointedly after a moment, because there was no more information forthcoming and because he was in no mood for riddles.

"Specialist Doyle, your presence is immediately required by those who have the power and authority to require it."

"Do I get to know who that might be—" he squinted to read the name tag through sleep-blurred eyes "—Guthrie?"

"Sergeant Beltran," he said. "But it came from higher up than that."

"Like how high?"

"Can't help you, hoss. I'm just the wheels. And haste would be good."

"Yeah, all right. Give me a minute."

"No problem—the lady downstairs is handing out chocolate-chip cookies," he said.

Doyle closed the door. He could hear Guthrie clumping down the stairs in search of Mrs. Bee. He stood for a moment, trying to figure this thing out. Surely Meehan hadn't made a complaint about him to his CO.

Surely.

He hobbled over to look out the window. Her car was gone.

So. She was at work.

So. She'd had the time to make a complaint if she was so inclined.

He'd told her the kiss thing was either the beginning or the end—and if she'd decided it was the end, having him hauled in would be pretty attention-getting, even for somebody as persistent as he was.

Still, it was Guthrie who'd showed up and not the MPs.

He got dressed in his standard invalid outfit and hobbled downstairs. Guthrie had Mrs. Bee treed, and she was happily handing out cookies.

"Let's go, Guthrie. See you later, Mrs. Bee," he said as he passed the kitchen door.

"Calvin?" she called as he stepped out on the porch. "You've got a steak dinner in here in the refrigerator."

Steak dinner?

"Katie brought it over this morning."

Yes!

"And, Calvin?" she called as he started down the steps. "I think you'd better get some cat litter."

"Right, Mrs. Bee," he said, trying not to collide with Guthrie who had decided to make his descent at the same time.

Okay. This is good. No MPs and a steak dinner in the fridge he thought as he made his way to Guthrie's "wheels." How upset can she be?

"Cat litter!" he said out loud.

"Looks like you're getting around better," Sergeant Beltran said when Doyle hobbled in.

"Roger that," Doyle said. "Or so they tell me."

"Okay, here's the deal. Guthrie here is going to take you over to the hospital. You call me here when you're done, and I'll see what I can scare up to get you back home."

"The hospital, Sergeant?" He'd seen all of hospitals he cared to—ever. It was all he could do to keep his follow-up appointments, much less drop into one out of the blue.

"Some big-deal surgeon from that hospital you were in out in Texas. He wants to review your X-rays or something."

He doesn't need me for that, Doyle almost said before he remembered that this wasn't a situation that required his input. He'd been summoned, apparently by a doctor who couldn't believe he was still kicking—sort of.

He rode to the hospital in silence, only half listening to Guthrie's chatter. He was more interested in considering his chances of running into Meehan—zero—and what he would say if he did—nothing. It was all up to her now—unless he couldn't take the waiting. Twisting in the wind was not his style.

He expected to be shuffled off to some waiting area for who knew how long, but he didn't expect that the hot-shot surgeon would be wanting more X-rays. That took all morning. And then it took all afternoon. He was hungry and more than a little ill-tempered by the time he actually saw the doctor face-to-face. He didn't remember the man at all, not his name or his face. He didn't remember much of anything before he was sent back here to recuperate.

"It looks surprisingly good, Specialist," the man said, briefly flashing an X-ray film in the air.

"Sir, yes, sir," Doyle said, in spite of the very big *but* he could feel coming.

"You could use a tune-up, though," the doctor continued, and Doyle realized he'd been holding his breath.

"Tune-up, sir?"

"The subsequent surgeries have considerably improved the degree of damage to the femur and tibia in your left leg, but see this here—and here?" he said, holding up the film again.

Doyle didn't see a damned thing.

"We can fix that without too much trouble."

"Trouble for who, sir?" Doyle asked, and the man grinned.

"Yes. I see what you mean. Well, it will be similar surgery to what you've had in the past, and it would have to be done in Texas."

"Sir, I don't want to do that. I'm just getting to the point where I can halfway get around again. I don't want to start over."

"It's going to save you a lot of trouble in the long run. And I think it will cut down on the pain."

"Sir, yes, sir. I understand that. But I—" He stopped and drew a sharp breath. More surgery. It was one thing to have it when you were so far gone you didn't care, and an altogether different deal when you weren't. The old make-it-hurt-more-so-it-will-hurt-less thing again.

"Sir, are we talking about surgery right away? Couldn't we just let it ride for a while? Let me see how far back I can come first? Maybe I won't need it."

The man stared at him. "You realize how lucky you are, Doyle. I didn't think you'd be walking again at all."

"Sir, yes, sir."

"There is a risk of losing what you've managed to regain if you let it go too long—but I understand your reluctance. I...think we can let it wait a month or so. The doctors here can follow you, make sure you're maintaining your current status."

"Yes, sir. Thank you, sir."

Doyle stood and left the room, trying to look like he was doing better than he actually was and not hobble. He walked into the crowded corridor, dodging patients in wheelchairs and staff in a hurry, barely seeing any of them.

Surgery.

Again.

Ah, damn!

The long day was taking its toll. He made it as far as he could before he had to stop and give in to the pain. He was supposed to call Sergeant Beltran about getting a ride home, but he didn't. He had his own plans for that.

He got onto the elevator and pushed the button for the floor where Meehan worked. He halfway expected not to find her—he'd been on a search for her at work before, but he saw her as soon as he got off the elevator, walking away from him in the opposite direction. His legs were killing him. It was as if knowing that things weren't right made the pain worse. There was no place to sit down so he stood, leaning hard into his cane, hoping the shakiness would pass and that Meehan would come back this way so he didn't have to go hunting for her. People walked past him, but he must have looked all right, he thought, because none of them paid him any attention.

"You okay, buddy?" a medic finally asked.

"I'm waiting for—Kate Meehan," he said around the pain. He tried shifting his weight, but it didn't help. It never helped.

The medic was watching him closely.

"And I'm a little...rough around the edges," Doyle confessed in the hope of getting the guy to get his ass in gear and go find her.

"She's here someplace," the medic said.

The medic walked away, intercepting Meehan when she came out of a room at the other end of the hall. Doyle saw her listen to whatever it was he told her, watched her look in his direction when the medic pointed him out. She said something to the medic and went back into the room. His unexpected appearance didn't rattle her, he'd say that for her. And either the medic was coming to help or to give him hell.

"She said wait," the medic said in passing.

"No problem," Doyle said, because he didn't

think he could manage anything else. He wasn't absolutely sure he could keep standing.

He looked down at the floor and tried to think of something besides the pain.

"Well, this looks familiar," Meehan said, catching him unaware. "You've done it again, haven't you?"

He knew what "it" meant. Yes, he'd walked too much. Yes, he'd gone without eating. Yes, he'd "let" his leg muscles go into spasm. He made no attempt to deny her very astute medical assessment. He just ignored it.

"I'm looking for a ride home," he said. "If I can't get one with you, I'll go to Plan B."

"Which is?"

"I can call Sergeant Beltran. He said he'd scare up somebody."

"You just happened to be in the neighborhood?"

"Downstairs. I've been…here all…day."

"Why?"

"Surgical consultation, I guess you'd call it—the guy who did the first operations in Texas wanted to see me. I got an early wake-up call for it."

"So what did the surgeon say?"

He sighed instead of answering. "So can I get a ride?" he asked, for once avoiding her eyes.

"It'll be about twenty-five or thirty minutes before I'm done here."

"No problem," he said.

"Oh, I can see that," she assured him. "Hampton, roll that wheelchair down here."

"I don't need—"

He stopped because he was getting the nurse look—the one he knew better than to tangle with. Besides that, he just wasn't up to having any kind of altercation about it.

Hampton, the medic, rolled the wheelchair front and center, and Doyle sat down in it. He hated wheelchairs. He'd logged more time in a wheelchair than he cared to remember. Long, empty, pain-filled days, and even longer nights.

But he sat down. He managed to get the footrests unfolded and to roll himself out of the traffic pattern and down to the windows at the end of the hall— where he could see out if he happened to get tired of watching Meehan working.

Unfortunately, he hurt too bad to do either. Hampton came by again, this time bearing a cold soft drink in a can and a pack of salted peanuts.

"Courtesy of herself," he said, handing them over.

Doyle took them. His hands shook so when he opened the peanuts, he spilled a number of them in his lap and on the floor. He was so hungry, he hardly tasted them. By the time Meehan appeared in the hall again, he was feeling better. Less starved, anyway. For food, that is.

He tossed the empty can and the peanut pack into the trash—and watched Meehan approaching. She looked great. If she'd been upset about last night, he didn't think it was enough to cause her to lose sleep.

"Okay," she said. "Do you want to go for 'tough' and walk to the parking lot or do you want to ride to the front door?"

"Tough," he said, using everything he had to get out of the chair. This was one of the things he liked about her. She'd give him the option of biting the bullet or making a fool of himself—up to a point.

She stood close to him when he was ready to start out, but she didn't say anything. He took a chance and put his hand on her shoulder.

"Thanks for the refreshments," he said.

"No problem."

They walked to the elevators, right by where people could see them. He didn't know how it looked—his holding on to her like that. He didn't care, but he thought she might. If she did, it didn't show.

"So what did the surgeon say?" she asked again as they got into the elevator.

"He wants to fix some things that don't suit him."

"And?"

"And I don't think I can stand it again."

She glanced at him. "Might help."

"Might not," he answered.

"How many times have you had surgery?" she asked.

"Eleven," he said, and she nodded.

He had let go of her in the elevator, but he rested

his hand on her shoulder again when they were walking toward the main entrance.

"That way," she said when they stepped outside.

The sun went behind a random cloud, but it was still hot. He struggled along, determined not to mention last night unless she did.

"You can wait here and I'll bring the car around."

"No," he said. The last thing he wanted was to give up touching her. He didn't care how much walking hurt.

She started to say something more, but three Black Hawks came over, the loud noise they made discouraging the attempt. He looked up, his heart beginning to pound—not with the pain of remembering but with pride. He followed their progress for a long time.

He glanced at Kate. She was watching him closely.

"I love that sound," he said. "Even after—"

He didn't finish the sentence, and she didn't ask him to.

He made it to the car, and they rode home in silence. He glanced at her from time to time, but if she ever looked at him, he didn't catch her at it. She stared straight ahead, eyes fixed on the road and the traffic—while he kept thinking about the kiss, the way her mouth had felt against his, the way she had tasted. All he could think about was putting his hands on her again.

When she pulled the car into her driveway and parked, he didn't hang around. He thanked her for the ride and got out.

"Doyle," she called when he'd gone a few steps.

He looked at her.

"What do you want?"

He knew exactly what she meant, and he wasn't going to pretend that he didn't. "I want everything, Kate," he said. "But I'll take whatever I can get."

She didn't say anything. He waited as long as he dared, then started for Mrs. Bee's again.

"You want to go someplace?" she called after him, when he'd all but given up hope.

"What...now?"

"Later. After I change. If you feel up to it."

"I feel up to it," he said, looking into her eyes. "I could use a little R and R after today."

Is this it? he thought. Is this the green light?

She suddenly smiled. "Don't you want to know where?"

"Not particularly," he said.

"Uncle Patrick's place," she said anyway.

"Ah, yes. Uncle Patrick. You're not going to hurt him, are you?"

"Not unless I have to."

"Well that's good to know."

"You'll like Uncle Patrick's place."

"Yeah? Why?"

"He's got a great menu and the waitresses wear really short skirts," she said. "The only thing is they're all Mrs. Bee's age,'' she added with a straight face.

''Probably can't run too fast, huh?''

''Probably not.''

The smile he was holding on to got away from him. ''I'd better rest up, anyway. See you later,'' he said, walking away, his heart lighter than it had been...

Ever.

He had no idea where this was going—or if it was going—but the door was open, and for now that was all he wanted.

Heat and eat, he decided as he made it up the steps into Mrs. Bee's house. It worked as well as anything to get past the pain. He didn't see Mrs. Bee anywhere, but he went into her refrigerator after his steak dinner, anyway. He took it upstairs and immediately ate half of it. Then he took a shower and shaved and fired up the heated throw and dozed until Kate came to get him.

He still wasn't to the point where he actually expected her to show up, and it occurred to him that he might never be. He knew she was beyond his reach by anyone's standards—which only meant that the situation was more in keeping with his military training. It had ''hunt the hill, get the hill'' written all over it.

He smiled to himself, wondering what Rita would say about all this.

No, he knew what she'd say.

No guts, no glory, Bugs, honey.

Kate arrived wearing a dress. Not *the* dress, but one just as interesting. This one was pale yellow and equally summery looking. A peasant dress, he thought it was called. She was wearing it off the shoulder. It had one wide ruffle so you couldn't see into the arm holes—with elastic in the top to make it stay where she put it. It made him think of beaches and girls going back and forth on the boardwalk, all fresh and clean after they'd spent the day lying in the sun and playing in the surf.

And the Kate Meehan version of this concept took his breath away.

"Is the pain any better?" she asked without prelude.

"Is there such a thing?" he asked, putting considerable effort into not leering. "Better pain?"

"You tell me."

"It's better."

"Let's go, then."

"Can we stop at the grocery store? Mrs. Bee wants some cat litter."

"She doesn't have a cat."

"I know that. You may not believe it, but with sergeants, certain nurses and Mrs. Bee, it's a whole lot easier to just get with the program. So how far are we going to have to travel to jack up Uncle Patrick?"

"Chapel Hill. Takes a little over two hours—for most people."

"I don't know if I like the sound of that."

"Sure you do. All you professional bullet stoppers live for danger."

"The key word here being *live*."

She did make it in under two hours—even with the stop for Mrs. Bee's nonexistent cat—not because she drove fast so much as she drove smart. She knew all kinds of back roads and she took every one of them. He wouldn't have been surprised if they'd cut through somebody's barn on the way to cutting through their corn field.

It made for an interesting trip, though. They kept the conversation light, well away from the five-hundred-pound gorilla that was last night's kiss sitting in the front seat every mile of the way. He had to work hard not to be distracted. He could see too much of her bare legs, for one thing. And her shoulders.

Neck.

"What?" she asked once when he sighed too loudly.

Uncle Patrick's place had a bright-blue door—and no parking lot. It was located on a side street, apparently with the idea of being accessible to the pedestrian college crowd. Kate eventually found a place to park, but the walk to the pub was long.

Very long.

He could feel her looking at him as they made their way down the brick sidewalk.

"Don't say it," he warned her, because she'd

wanted to put him out in front while she circled the block. He might have let her if he'd known it was going to be this much of a trip. At the time, the choice had been walking or standing and waiting—both painful.

"I'm not going to say anything—except don't pick any fights with the college boys."

"Who me?"

"It's been known to happen," she said.

"In case you haven't noticed, I'm not exactly up to fisticuffs with anybody. Except you, maybe."

"Very funny. I'm just telling you. The haircut may stand out in here, so don't get all testy."

"I'll try," he said, and she gave him a look.

"I will," he insisted.

She didn't look particularly reassured.

The place was much more crowded than he expected. It was still early by pub standards, and it was July. Somehow he'd thought the college crowd mostly left town in the summer. The establishment certainly looked like a pub—all dark wood, high-backed booths, assorted tables for two and a long bar. It smelled like a pub, too. He could immediately identify at least one item on the chalkboard menu—leek soup. His grandmother had made leek soup.

There was a small raised stage in the corner. A band of scruffy-looking musicians were crowded onto it and playing raucous Celtic music that spilled out onto the sidewalk every time someone opened the door.

And, even knowing that Kate had been pulling his chain, he still looked for the Mrs. Bee-like waitresses in miniskirts. He didn't see any waitresses at all—but he saw Uncle Patrick.

"Katie, darlin'!" the man bellowed from behind the bar. "Come here, come here! I need you!"

"Uncle Patrick, I want you to meet somebody," she yelled over the din. "This is Doyle. His friends call him—"

"Cal," Doyle said to Uncle Patrick over the heads of the guys lined up at the bar. If Kate wanted him to behave, there was no point in throwing a nickname like Bugs out for Joe College to jump all over.

"Welcome to Paddy's, Cal," Uncle Patrick said. "Katie, darlin', will you help me now?"

"What can I do, Uncle Pat?"

Uncle Patrick was already motioning her to come around to his side of the bar. He immediately pinned a towel around her waist and dubbed her a bartender. To Doyle's surprise, Kate fell right in, taking orders and filling frosted mugs with draft beer. She brought him the first one.

"Goldie's late," she said, apparently to explain her new job. "Can you grab a seat someplace?" She carefully offered him the mug.

He had to part a few of the bar crowd so he could sit down on the only empty stool. As predicted, the haircut was an object of interest—he could feel eyes on his head—and his legs and walking cane. This particular bunch had the good sense not to comment, but one of them kept staring.

"Sometimes you hit the ground," Doyle said to him. "Sometimes the ground hits you."

The comment was completely lost on him, and he turned back to his friends.

The music stopped and immediately started up again, this time with a fiddle solo. Uncle Patrick bustled around, laughing and waiting tables, clearly a man in his element. Doyle used the opportunity to watch Kate.

Damn, he thought. She is so fine.

And he wasn't the only one who recognized it. She also knew her way around a beer tap.

"Two beers!" a young punk standing next to Doyle yelled at her as she moved down the bar with her hands full of mugs. She gave a short nod to show him that he'd heard him.

"I bet she gives great head," he said to his buddy as Kate went past again.

Don't do it, Doyle thought. He's just being cute for his buddies.

The punk made another remark, one which Doyle didn't hear but which his friends all appreciated. The kid was getting all pumped up here. Unfortunately, the Rules of Engagement were crystal clear. No picking fights with the college crowd.

Doyle took a swallow of beer. It was cold and icy just like he liked it—but his whole arm ached with wanting to jerk the kid off his feet and sling him over the bar.

He only heard part of the next remark. "—knee pads."

Let it go. Let it go....

Kate brought the punk his beers, and instead of handing her the money, he made a grab for the elastic in the top of the yellow ruffle, clearly intending to pull it out and stuff the money down the front of her dress. Doyle's hand shot out before he even thought about it, knocking over the beers and grabbing the punk's forearm, twisting hard and bringing him around so that they were face-to-face.

"I am going to tell you this one time and one time only, son. Keep your hands where they belong. You understand me?"

The punk was clearly in a state of disbelief— things like this didn't happen to him. Up until now, he'd obviously had a free hand to do and say whatever he pleased to the hired help, no matter where he happened to find himself. He was trying hard to bluff it out, trying to pretend the grip on his arm didn't hurt as much as Doyle knew it did.

"Do you understand me!" Doyle said again.

"Yeah," the punk said finally. "I understand."

"Good," Doyle said, letting him go. He glanced at Kate. The entire brief incident hadn't caused any disruption in the place. People still laughed and talked. The fiddler still sawed away on his fiddle. But she was mad—at him, not the punk.

She got the punk two more beers.

"I can take care of myself!" she said after the college kid had taken them and gone.

"I know that. I just happened to be closer."

She started to say something else, then didn't. She went back to tending bar. He sat there and nursed his beer, totally out of sorts. What was he supposed to do? Let the guy jerk her clothes half off her in the middle of a pub?

"I didn't even swear," he said under his breath.

"Cal!"

He looked around. Uncle Patrick was motioning for him to come sit in a nearby booth. He picked up his beer and hobbled over.

"I appreciate what you did for Katie just now," Uncle Patrick said as he sat down.

"I'm glad somebody does, sir," Doyle said.

"Ah, well. You know our Katie is a bit touchy about having to depend on people."

Doyle didn't say anything to that. Uncle Patrick stared at him across the table, clearly with something else on his mind.

"So you would be him, then?" he said after a time.

"Sir?"

"The lad who has the Meehan girls all in an uproar. Of course, some of them are more in an uproar than others are," he said, nodding in Kate's direction. "You're in the army, are you?"

"Yes, sir."

"Can you stay in—in the shape you're in?"

"They'll find something for me, sir, if I want it."

"Ah, but will you be happy at it?"

"Don't know, sir," Doyle said, watching Kate at work behind the bar, a fact that didn't escape her uncle's notice.

"I don't think he'll be bothering her again tonight," Uncle Patrick said.

Doyle took another swallow of beer. "I expect there's more where he came from."

"You know, lad, I've been in an uproar about you myself."

"I don't know what to say to that, sir."

"Say nothing at all—because I'm more at ease about you and Katie now I've met you. Of course, that doesn't mean I won't kick your arse if you should ever happen to need it."

"Understood, sir," Doyle said, lifting his beer mug in a salute to the old man.

"I hear you're a bit of a musician," Uncle Patrick said, taking Doyle by surprise.

"I wouldn't go that far, sir."

"That's not what Katie told me. We'll be having an open mike tonight before long. I expect to see you up there. Now, it's back to work for me. No rest for the weary. It's been a pleasure to meet you, lad."

"You, too, sir. Sir, there is one other thing."

"What's that, lad?"

"Could you watch your diet—take better care of yourself? I think the Meehan girls would appreciate it."

The old man laughed and walked away.

Doyle stayed in the booth, listening to the music and still watching Kate, the very real possibility of more surgery jabbing at the edges of his mind.

Texas.

He didn't even have the prospect of being a patient on her floor again. He kept wondering what else she had told her family about him. To say that he was surprised that she'd discussed him with her uncle Patrick would be a major understatement. Of course, from what he knew of the family, she had probably had no choice but to give up some information about him.

Every now and then she looked in his direction—to see if he was staying out of trouble probably.

A waitress came in the door. He knew that because of the short skirt. And because she may have had a couple of years on Mrs. Bee. She was met with an enthusiastic "Gold-dee" chant and a round of applause from the regulars—which she acknowledged with a little quickstep, then got immediately to work.

Kate was relieved of her bartending duties, but it was a while before she came over to the booth. She took the opportunity to talk to her uncle first. Doyle thought she was making her case about his taking care of himself and not worrying the rest of them. Eventually she walked in Doyle's direction.

"You ready to go?" she asked him.

"Already?"

"If you stay, you're going to have to sing," she said.

"In that case we better hop and pop. I can tell you right now I know how to clear a room."

She waited for him to get to his feet. She was close enough for him to put his hand on her shoulder when they walked toward the door, but he didn't. He was trying his damnedest not to mess up here—and it wasn't easy.

"You still mad at me?" he asked when they were outside and walking toward the car—because he couldn't leave well enough alone. "You might as well know I'd do it again," he said when she didn't answer him.

She stopped walking and looked at him. "It's not going to work, you know that."

People walked by them. He barely noticed.

"What's not going to work?"

"You and me."

"How do you know? Stranger things have happened. Some things you don't plan, Kate. You just go with them—and see what happens."

She sighed and began walking again toward where she'd parked the car.

"Kate," he said when she'd gone a few steps.

She looked back at him.

"You're my—"

He stopped because Joe College and his friends were walking by. The punk gave Doyle the go-to-hell-slash-another-day-another-time look as he passed—

Doyle expected no less—but the kid didn't say anything, probably because his friends had convinced him that he would be the better man by *not* taking on a gimp. But he'd learned his lesson on at least one account. He didn't pay any attention to Kate whatsoever.

She waited for Doyle to catch up.

"What were you going to say?" she asked. "I'm your what?"

"Nothing," he said, losing his nerve.

She stood looking at him.

"I...wasn't mad because you took on that kid," she said after a moment. "I was mad because I was *glad* you did it."

"I don't think I understand—but that's okay."

"I don't know what to do and I hate it," she said.

"Do about what?"

"About you!"

"How hard can it be?" he asked. "You either let me hang around or you tell me to take a hike." He started walking again, and after a moment she followed.

"Tell me what you were going to say," she said when she caught up. "I'm your what?"

"Fantasy," he answered, this time without hesitation. "You're my fantasy."

Chapter Nine

She didn't ask him about it until they were riding down a narrow country back road in the moonlight.

"What is it?"

He gave a quiet sigh of relief that she was still talking to him and looked in her direction. He didn't want to be coy. And he didn't want to be forthcoming, either.

"I don't want to tell you," he said, opting for the pure, unadulterated truth.

"Why not?"

"I don't think it's a good idea."

"Why not?" she asked again.

"Because I don't want to come across like that punk in the bar—and I don't want to end up walking back to Fayetteville."

She slowed the car to make a turn onto another secondary road. The moon hung directly in front of them now, making the road a silvery pathway.

"This fantasy—does it involve…food?"

"Food? No—" he said, wondering where in the world she got that idea.

"Sex, then."

"That would be it."

"I see."

She didn't say anything else for a long time. He shifted his position in the seat, more to keep his mind off how close she was to him than anything else. He definitely needed something to do, so he wouldn't try to touch her. He really wanted to touch her.

"Where?" she asked.

"What?" he said, startled.

"Where does this fantasy take place?"

"I don't know," he said—which was the truth.

"Okay, then. When?"

"Don't know."

She glanced at him. "This doesn't sound like much of a fantasy."

"Guys don't waste time on logistic assessment, Meehan. There's no where and no when. There's especially not a why. We only do the who and what. Most of the time just the what."

"Interesting. No frills. Cut to the chase."

"Pretty much," he said, hoping he was off the hook now.

"And this particular chase would involve…what?"

He sighed. She was deliberately giving him a hard time here, and she knew it.

"You keep this up and I'm going to tell you."

"Go ahead."

"I don't want to have to walk to Fayetteville," he said again.

"I promise I won't put you out."

"Yeah, you say that *now*."

"Tell me!"

"Okay!" he said, accepting the challenge. "We are more or less horizontal."

"And?"

"And you want to."

"To…?"

"To," he assured her.

"Well, I would, wouldn't I?" she said. "In *your* fantasy."

"Right. You want to—and I don't."

She looked at him. Even in the dark, he could read her that'll-be-the-day expression.

"Any particular reason for your…reluctance?"

"I'm playing hard to get," he said. "Don't worry, though. You talk me into it."

"And how do I do that?"

"With everything you got."

She laughed. She couldn't be mad if she laughed. Or so he thought.

Hoped.

She didn't say anything else—she just chuckled to herself every now and then.

He sighed. Whatever reaction he might have expected, mirth wasn't it. It wasn't even on the list.

When she finally pulled into her driveway, he was totally ready for the moment of truth. This was it as far as he was concerned—the beginning or the end, and he was going to tell her so. She got out of the car before he could stop her, and she stood looking up at the night sky.

He struggled to get out, and he hobbled to stand next to her. "Are you going to say anything or not?" he asked.

"About what?"

"About the situation," he said with a good deal more patience than he felt.

She looked at him...for a long time. He waited. This was absolutely it, and they both knew it. He could hear the faint tinkling of wind chimes, smell the lemon fragrance from the mystery plant on the patio. He wondered if she had any idea how beautiful she was or how much being even this close to her affected him.

"Are you?" he asked again.

She gave a quiet sigh and looked up at the starry sky again.

"Kate?"

She looked back at him. "Your place or mine?" she asked quietly.

"Yours," he said without missing a beat. Because

he realized suddenly that his fantasy had a ''where'' after all. Her bed.

Her bed.

She walked off toward the patio, leaving him standing. He hesitated, then hobbled along after her. When he entered the house, he didn't see her at first. He found her in the kitchen, opening an MRE for the cat. She emptied it into a small bowl and carried the bowl into the side room where she kept the washer and dryer, closing the door firmly after the cat went inside.

She walked past him into another room, leaving him standing again. He made no attempt to follow her. He simply waited.

''Do you have condoms?'' she asked matter-of-factly when she came back. He could feel the effort it was taking for her to look at him.

''No,'' he said.

''Doesn't matter. I have some— What?'' she asked abruptly, as if he'd made some remark or had some reaction to the fact that she practiced safe sex if the occasion happened to arise.

''Nothing,'' he said, looking at her. She avoided his eyes.

''Okay, then,'' she said, meaning to get by him. He caught her hand.

''Hold it,'' he said.

''What?

''Just stand there.''

''Why?''

"Just stand still. I want to say this one thing—" He let his cane lean against the table and put his hands on her shoulders, because he thought she'd take off if he didn't. She didn't try to get way, but that was about all he could say for it. "Don't," he said, looking into her eyes.

"Don't what?"

"Don't act like you're open for business and like this doesn't mean anything to me. I've been posted here a long time. If all I wanted was to get laid, I know where to go. Understand?"

She didn't say anything.

"Understand?" he asked again.

She nodded, but she wasn't happy about having to address the topic.

"And try not to look at me like I'm the worst thing that could ever have happened to you."

"You are," she said.

"No, I'm not. It's going to be good—you and me. You'll see."

Whatever comment she might have wanted to make got lost in a sigh.

"Get ready," he said. "I'm going to kiss you now, so don't panic."

"I never panic."

"Right." His arms slid around her, but he didn't do anything. "This is not good," he said because she was standing so stiffly. "You're ready to run."

"No, I'm not."

"Yes, you are."

"Okay, I am," she confessed.

"Close your eyes," he said.

She didn't do it.

"Close them," he repeated.

When she did, he kissed her gently on the forehead, then her cheek, first one, then the other.

"How was that?"

"It was…fine…good," she said.

"Too easy, right? No problem."

"No problem."

He tightened his arms around her, bringing her closer, so that her head rested against his shoulder.

"I want you so bad," he said against her ear. "So—" he kissed the corner of her mouth "—bad…"

He kissed her for real then, and he meant to hold back, to go slow, but he couldn't do it.

He was never going to get enough of this woman. Never.

She returned the kiss. Nothing about it was one-sided. He was bombarded by more sensations than he could register. She smelled so good and she tasted so good. He wanted to do everything with her, to her. His hands slid over her body in a search for bare skin. He pulled at her skirt until he could get his hand up under it, and he pressed her body into his. She was clinging to him. His knees had gone weak. It was all he could do to keep his balance.

"Where's the bedroom?" he said urgently. "Where—"

She stepped away from him, but she held on to his hand and led him down a narrow hallway. He followed as best he could, reeling, drunk with desire.

Her bedroom was at the end of the hall. A small lamp burned on the nightstand. The bed was big. She pulled the bedspread back, but that was all he gave her time to do. He sat down heavily on the side of the bed and lay back, bringing her with him. He kissed her, again and again—deep, open-mouthed kisses that made him feel as if he was going to explode. His hands slid into her hair, pulling out the pins so that it tumbled down onto her shoulders. And how long had he wanted to do that?

He suddenly leaned back so that he could see her face. "Tell me what I can do. I don't want to hurt you," he said, and she caught his hand and placed it firmly on her breast.

"You won't," she said, looking into his eyes.

He didn't need any more invitation than that. He kissed her again, touching her now the way he wanted. With her help, he moved up farther on the bed. She pulled his shirt up and over his head and tossed it aside, then reached for her dress.

"Let me do it," he said. His hands trembled, but he managed. The dress. The bra—lacy, definitely see-through. The "pants" she'd rightly accused him of wanting to get into.

He ran his hands over her body, and he looked. At her breasts. At the surgical scar on the left one above the nipple. He touched her all over, savored and tasted her until her head arched back and she gave a soft moan. Her fingers dug into his shoulders. She was so beautiful. He couldn't believe his incredible luck. This woman—this beautiful, beautiful woman—wanted *this*.

Wanted him.

"Wait," she whispered, attempting to pull down the sheet and arrange the pillows.

"No," he said. "I can't. Not…this time—"

He couldn't wait. It was all he could do to last until he could get the rest of his clothes off and the condom pack opened. He had to grit his teeth at the feel of her hands on him.

Kate!

Then he brought her astride him and thrust deeply into her, losing himself in the intense pleasure of her body, a pleasure he could die from. He wanted to tell her how good it was, but he couldn't.

Lost.

He was lost, and he never wanted to be found again.

Everything was happening so fast. It was going to end too quickly. He was too far gone for restraint.

He wrapped his arms tightly around her as he reached his noisy and unrestrained climax. She collapsed against him, spent, and he kissed whatever he could reach, his breathing ragged, his body exhausted. When she would have moved away from him, he kept her where she was. He didn't want it to be over. Not yet.

Not yet—

She lay on top of him, and after a while he rolled her onto the bed so that she could stretch out beside him. He brushed her hair back from her face because he wanted to see her eyes.

They were so sad.

"I didn't hurt you, did I?" he asked. "I didn't mean—"

She pressed her fingertips against his lips. "You didn't hurt me."

He didn't quite believe her.

She suddenly smiled. "Well," she said, giving a long sigh. "So much for playing hard to get."

He slept the sleep of a happy, satisfied man—and he woke up cold, hungry and alone. He didn't know where he was at first—an all-too-familiar response for someone who had fallen asleep in as many strange places as he had. But then he remembered. He would remember for as long as he lived.

He turned over painfully so he could see the clock.

Oh-five-twenty.

Maybe she had to go in to work again, he thought, listening for some sound of her in the house. But he would have heard the phone if it had rung, surely.

Maybe she'd had second thoughts about all this and she'd moved to some other part of the house to get away from him. He managed to sit up on the side of the bed and get his shorts on, and then to get to his feet. He had no idea what he'd done with the cane. Kitchen, maybe. That was the last place he remembered having it.

He struggled to the bathroom, and he had to hold on to the wall to get there. He still didn't see Kate anywhere and he didn't call out to her. The cat was waiting patiently by the door when he came out. It was clearly glad to see him, doing the ballet turns again and then escorting him the rest of the way into the kitchen. It went directly to the kitchen cabinet where the packets of cat food were kept.

"No way, chow hound," he said. "I know when you got fed last."

His cane was leaning against the kitchen table. He took it and walked to the back door, then onto the patio. To his surprise the cat came with him outside—a decision it regretted almost immediately. It shot under the potting table and assumed a panicked crouch. Kate's car was conspicuously absent from the driveway where she'd left it.

Doyle stood staring at the empty spot, breathing in the cool morning air as if that was all he'd come out here for.

Okay, Kate. Now what?

Clearly she saw this situation as a one-night stand, and she was behaving accordingly. It wasn't the first time she'd disappeared when he was asleep in her house, but the other time she'd at least left some reasonably informative notes so he'd have some idea about what he was supposed to do.

So where is she?

There were no birds stirring yet. No sounds at all except an occasional vehicle passing on a distant, more heavily traveled street. It occurred to him after a moment that it was daylight enough for some-one—Mrs. Bee—to see him standing outside in his underwear. The notion didn't bother him enough to make him go back into the house.

The cat suddenly jumped up on the table and leaned in his direction.

"What?" he said, reaching out to briefly scratch its ears. "Is the coast clear now?"

A sudden spasm in the muscles in his right leg caused him to grab the edge of the table. The cat scattered, jumping at the back door as if it expected it to open like the ones at the grocery store.

"Ah, *damn!*" he said, bending lower. It was clear that the sudden and spectacular resurrection of his sex life had done nothing for the rest of what ailed him. And the more the pain escalated, the more real the prospect of yet another surgery became. Lieu-tenant McGraw had come almost all the way back, but he didn't have the same kind of damage, and Doyle might as well get adjusted to that fact. He could see the rest of his life turning into one trip to the operating room after another. He did *not* want to go to damn Texas!

He leaned against the table, breathing deeply, at war with his own body, struggling to get the upper hand. After a moment he was able to make it as far as the door to let the still-freaked-out cat back inside.

A car pulled into the driveway, and he turned to look, still holding the door open. Kate parked in her same spot and got out. She was wearing khaki shorts and a little white T-shirt and carrying a white paper bag. He was immediately aware of two things—how glad he was to see her, and, unless he was very mistaken, how glad *she* was to see *him*.

More than he expected. Maybe more than she expected.

"Are you *trying* to upset the neighbors?" she asked, gesturing toward his boxer shorts and the neighborhood in general.

"Nah. I was hoping your sisters would drop by."

"Oh, please. I'm not ready for that."

"Have you got to work today?"

"No."

"Outstanding," he said.

She stopped in front of him, awkward suddenly, as if she'd just found herself in completely strange terrain and she wasn't at all sure what direction she should take. He couldn't stop staring at her, and he couldn't stop remembering. He was remembering so well that she suddenly blushed—or he thought she did.

"I brought breakfast," she said in an attempt to hide it. She held up the bag.

"Some other time," he said, opening the door wider so she could go inside.

She didn't go, and he took the bag from her and gave it a toss. It landed...somewhere.

"Don't you want to know what it is?" she said, trying not to smile.

"Later," he assured her, propelling her inside. "I have other, more pressing matters to take care of."

"Like what?" she asked, her eyes full of mischief.

"Like—" He stopped because the mischief in her eyes suddenly gave way to something else.

"What?" he asked, taking a step toward her. He expected her to back away, but she didn't.

"The truth?" she asked.

"Always," he said.

She took a breath. "All right. When I woke up, I thought I wanted you gone. I was going to tell you that when I got back—but I didn't expect to see you standing out here..."

"And?" he said, because she was on a roll with the bad news, and he might as well hear all of it.

She looked down at the floor, and whatever she said next, he didn't understand.

"What?"

She looked up at him. "I said, I keep losing my nerve."

"You don't need it. You don't have to tell me to take a hike. I'm getting the picture here."

"No—that's not what I wanted to say to you."

"What then?"

"Take me to bed," she said.

Just out with it. No frills and in plain English.

He stared at her, wondering if he looked as stunned as he felt.

"Okay," he said agreeably when he'd recovered, trying not to grin because she was so solemn.

"I know how crazy this all sounds," she said. "But I'm serious."

"So am I."

"This is *insane*," she said, coming to him and leaning her forehead against chest.

"Affirmative," he said, because he was beginning to pick up on the fact that being with her was going to be one hell of a roller-coaster ride.

He put his arms around her, anyway.

"It doesn't just *seem* insane. It *is* insane."

"Roger that," he said.

"People are going to talk."

"Roger that, too."

She leaned back to look at him. "You don't care," she said in a tone that couldn't have been more accusing.

"Not a damn bit," he said, letting the grin he'd been trying to hold back get away from him. He was one more happy man here.

"So which one of us is going to play hard to get this time?" he asked.

"I'm thirty-two," he said, because he didn't think she was asleep.

She opened her eyes. "Is this where I tell you how old I am?"

"I don't care how old you are. I just thought I'd mention it. In case you want to beat yourself up about the age thing some more."

"I'm not beating myself up," she said, closing her eyes again. "At the moment," she added. She stretched and gave a quiet sigh—while he appreciated the view. They had made love, eaten cold bacon biscuits, slept, showered, made love again.

And now he wanted to talk.

"Are you in love with the real estate guy?" he asked bluntly. He ran his finger along her collarbone to the soft swell of her breast with the fascination of a grateful and still-interested man.

"No," she said, her eyes still closed.

"You...sat out in the rain a long time."

"I have trust issues," she said. "I told you I misjudged him. It brought back a lot of old feelings— feelings I had when my marriage ended. For a while I just couldn't handle being that wrong. Again."

"He never noticed the scar?"

She opened her eyes. "Why are you asking me this?"

"It's a guy thing."

"Enlighten me."

"I want to know if you and the real estate guy were lovers and I'm trying to be suave about it."

She didn't say anything.

"So how am I doing?"

"Not good," she said.

"Were you lovers?"

"No," she said. "We weren't lovers."

"I hate his guts, anyway," he said, bringing her closer. "I even hate the bastard you bought the condoms for."

"You're the bastard I bought the condoms for."

He couldn't keep from grinning. "Yeah?"

"Yeah."

"Outstanding!"

"Cal! Cal…!"

"What—?"

"Wake up!"

"What?"

"Wake up!"

He opened his eyes. Kate was leaning over him, the way she had that night Mrs. Bee had dragged her out of the shower to come see about him.

"You were dreaming."

"I don't—what?"

"Are you awake now?"

"Yeah…yeah," he said, trying to calm his erratic breathing.

"Let me see," she said. "Look at me." Her warm hands cupped his face as she looked into his eyes.

"I'm okay," he said, trying to drag up enough of a smile to reassure her. "Sorry."

"Are you hurting?"

"Not much."

"You're not telling me the truth again."

"Okay, I hurt," he said.

"Let me get the throw."

"No," he said, grabbing her arm when she would have gotten out of bed. "I don't need it. I need—" He gritted his teeth against the latest onslaught of pain.

"What can I do?"

"Everything. Do everything. Take my...mind off it. Kate!"

"Shhh," she whispered, pressing her face against his. "It's all right." She moved closer to him and gently kissed his mouth. He immediately returned the kiss, giving himself over to the sensation, to losing himself in her.

"Kate..."

Chapter Ten

All three sisters stood on the doorstep.

"Where's is my sister?" Grace asked, and to hell with the pleasantries. He had the distinct impression that if his answer didn't suit her, it would be way too bad for him.

"She's at work," he said. "She won't get off until seventeen hundred."

"Then what are *you* doing here?"

"You don't want to go there, Grace. Trust me."

She and Arley frowned. Gwen beamed.

"I just don't know what you think you're doing," Grace said.

"Right now, I'm on my way home. Go on in. There's some iced tea in the refrigerator." He was pushing his luck by flaunting his familiarity with the available beverages in Kate's kitchen—but he just couldn't resist rattling their cages. The real truth here, though, was that he owed them. Their fake dinner invitation and their subsequent push to keep Kate from doing anything outrageous with him were the reasons she had been sitting on the patio alone in the dark in the first place. Not only had they given him the perfect opportunity to kiss her, they had also put her in the aggravated state of mind to let him— and he had no doubt that that kiss had led to the night and day he'd just had.

He stood back to let them in, then hobbled out the door. The cat came with him, and he didn't blame it. He expected that the atmosphere in the house was going to be anything but peaceful.

The cat escorted him across the yard, looking for coyotes all the way. When he opened Mrs. Bee's back door, it shot into the hallway before he could head it off.

"Sorry, Mrs. Bee," he said as the cat zipped past her. "Maybe I can bribe her back outside."

"It's okay, Calvin. We've got cat litter."

"Cat litter—I forgot to give you the cat litter."

"Katie brought it over."

"Oh," he said, wondering when she'd had the chance to do that.

"She came over to tell me," Mrs. Bee added.

"Tell you?"

"Where you were."

He tried to let it go, but he didn't make it two steps before he asked. "What did she say?"

"Oh, nothing much. Something about keeping you chained to her bed."

"Whoa! Mrs. Bee!" he said, more than a little taken aback by her candor. He could feel his ears get hot. He'd made it through the girlie-magazine thing, but she'd royally ambushed him this time.

"It's all right, Calvin," she said, stepping into the kitchen. "I've been around—and it's not that difficult to see how you and Katie feel about each other. That's how I knew we were going to need cat litter."

He didn't know how much Mrs. Bee could tell by looking at Kate, but *he* might as well be carrying a sign. "Mrs. Bee?" he called.

The old lady turned and looked at him.

"Thanks," he said.

"For what, Calvin?"

"For...not getting all pushed out of shape about Kate and me, I guess."

She smiled. "Love is where you find it, Calvin," she said. "And it's not to be wasted. Nobody knows that better than I do. The girls are coming later—in case you want to plan your day accordingly."

"Okay," he said, but then the light dawned.

"Mrs. Bee...what you just said. Does that mean the girls know about Kate and me?"

"Yes, Calvin," she said with the same kind of

gentleness she must have used on her students whenever they asked really dumb questions.

The old lady disappeared into the kitchen.

"Oh, great," he said under his breath. He didn't have the strength to engage the church ladies. To say that he was tired would have been an understatement. He had missed a lot of sleep in the last twenty-four hours, and he couldn't have been happier about it.

He looked at the stairs, took a deep breath and began the climb to the second floor. Halfway up, the cat joined him, wary of being in strange surroundings but sticking with him, anyway.

"If you didn't have friends in high places, you'd be out of here—you know that, don't you?" he said to it.

When he was inside his apartment, he looked out the window. The Meehan sisters' cars were still there. He supposed they were working themselves up to give Kate hell when she got home.

He toyed briefly with the idea of hunting up something to eat, then abandoned that for the lure of his bed. He lay down on top of the covers and fell immediately asleep. He was vaguely aware at some point that there was a thunderstorm passing over and that the cat wandered around investigating the perimeter. Neither event was enough to bring him completely awake. He slept on, eventually becoming aware that he was not alone. He opened his eyes and looked to his left. Kate was sleeping next to him, her head on the pillow. She was still wearing her nurse clothes. In fact, she still had her shoes on. Apparently, she'd arrived, assessed the situation and crashed.

He dropped off to sleep again, waking the next time because she stirred against him and put one arm around his waist.

"Hey," he said, and she opened her eyes.

"I'm hiding," she murmured sleepily.

"From the church ladies or the Meehan sisters?" he said, reaching to caress her cheek.

"Both," she said.

"Yeah, me, too."

"I'll wake up later, okay?"

"Take your time. I'm not going anywhere."

She went immediately back to sleep, and he turned on his side so he could look at her.

It was raining still. He could hear it on the roof. He was happy that she had come here, whatever the motivation, but he was by no means presuming anything. He felt closer to her than he'd ever been to another human being in his life—but he had no expectations. None. He was in it for as long as it was going to last—he knew that much. He might even tell her that at some point, but he wouldn't tell her the rest of it.

He picked up a tendril of her honey-colored hair and wrapped it around his finger.

I love you, Kate.

* * *

When she woke up, they went to the grocery store, right out in front of God and everybody, as if she didn't mind that people they both knew might see them together and conclude that what was happening between them was happening. It took a while to get the shopping done, and then to take groceries to her house to put a meal together. It struck him more than once how easy they were in each other's company. On the one hand, it was as if they'd been together for years. And, on the other hand, there was that red-hot undercurrent of still-unmet desire—and they'd only just touched the surface.

Late or not, the sisters insisted on staying for supper. All three of them. He didn't mind. They weren't any worse than any number of platoon sergeants he'd had. Kate ran the sisters out of the kitchen, and he did most of the food prep, parked on a bar stool.

"I hate cooking," Kate said, handing him another onion to chop.

"Why?"

"Because I had to do it all the time when I was at home. Grace had too much seniority to get stuck with it. Arley was too little. And Gwen would have burned the house down."

He didn't doubt it for an instant. "You're not sorry, are you?"

"What? That I didn't let Gwen burn the house down?"

"No. That they're all in an uproar—because of you and me."

She leaned against him for a moment, in spite of the fact that all three of the sisters could see her if they happened to look up from the intense, low-voiced conversation they were having in the den. "I'm not sorry."

He believed her...then and all through the meal that could have been more strained than it was if he'd taken the collective disapproval seriously. Kate's sisters were entitled to their opinions—but that was as far as he was willing to go.

He talked to all three of them, asked polite questions, pulled the answers out of them when he had to. He thought he liked Gwen the best. Gwen told him all about Kate when she was a little girl, the kind of things that would have embarrassed a lesser woman, the kind of things a sister might tell the man who mattered.

He also thought he understood the other two. Grace was worried about the big "What will people say?" And Arley...Arley was like a jealous little kid. He was taking up Kate's time and attention—cutting into the many hours she wanted devoted to *her* problems, and she did *not* appreciate it. She wanted Kate at the ready so she could pick up the pieces of her and Scottie's life as needed.

The meal was great—some kind of skillet beef, potato and onion thing. For someone who hated to cook, Kate did just fine, in his opinion. He couldn't keep his eyes off her, and he didn't care what the sisters thought about that. He was just barely able to keep his hands off her.

After the meal, he intended to help get the kitchen squared away, but he didn't have to have a house fall on him. The sisters were getting restless.

"Where's that awful cat?" he heard Grace ask.

"Kate said it moved in with Cal," Arley said.

"Figures," Grace said.

Kate looked up sharply at the remark.

"Go or stay?" he asked as she stacked another dirty plate and carried them to the kitchen counter.

She looked at him gratefully. "Go," she said.

He smiled. "Want me to loan you my whip and chair?"

"I've got my own," she said. "And I think I need to use them."

"Thanks for the meal," he said.

"You did most of the work."

He stood looking into her eyes.

"Could you hobble a little closer?" she asked. "I don't want you to think I'm easy."

He grinned...and hobbled.

She wanted the kiss to be as restrained and chaste as possible, because of the potential onlookers. He wanted the kiss to be deep and hard.

He won.

"See you later," he said, letting her go and hobbling again, this time in the direction of the back door. "Tell the sisters 'bye for me."

She followed him to the door, and he thought that

if he'd turned around at any point as he made his way across the yard, she would still be watching.

Life is good, he thought.

And it stayed good. He hadn't realized how alone he'd been or how much he would welcome another person in his life.

No. Not just another person. Kate Meehan.

Initially he had been determined not to crowd her, but she didn't seem to need the space he was willing to give her. He spent the time she was at work at his own place. The rest of the time—the nights—he spent with her. After the initial struggle she'd had, he marveled at the ease with which she now seemed to accept whatever was happening between them. If it still mattered to her what her family or anyone else thought about it, he couldn't tell.

He loved being with her, and that was the bottom line. It wasn't just the sexual satisfaction she gave him. It was everything else as well. He liked looking at her. He liked talking to her. Naturally, he felt no hesitation about bringing up whatever topic he wanted to know about.

"Tell me about this," he said one night in bed, gently touching the surgical scar. She looked into his eyes before she answered—for what he didn't know. Reassurance that it wasn't just morbid curiosity on his part, he supposed.

"They found something when I had a routine mammogram," she said. "It was in the early stage.

I had a lumpectomy and radiation. It was the first time I've ever really been sick."

"And you're still mad about it," he suggested, because he thought he knew her well enough to guess that.

"Yes," she said, giving him a surprised look. "I'm the strong one in the family. I fix everybody else's problems—I didn't know how to have one of my own. Not that kind, anyway."

"So how did you get that job—fixing everybody else's problems?"

"I'm not sure. I think I must like it on some level or I wouldn't do it."

"Did you get along with your mom and dad?"

"Mom, yes. Dad, no," she said, moving so that she could rest her head on his shoulder.

"Why not?"

"I don't know why not. Do you know why you didn't get along with yours?"

"Sure. He wasn't around after I was six months old."

"Your mother was around. Why didn't you get along with her?"

He had to think about that. The remark took him by surprise—until he remembered that he had been a patient on her ward. She would know that no one came to see him except Rita. She might have even been part of some Chain-of-Concern thing that tried to find out why. "Okay, I see your point," he said after a moment, and the conversation turned to other things.

Many other things. Since he'd been in the army, he had been on a very prolonged quest for higher education. He hadn't gotten as far as John Galsworthy in his studies, but he had his opinions about the things he had learned, and he could hold up his end of an intelligent discussion now and then.

He needed to be able to do that—to keep himself occupied so he wouldn't ruin things. Kate had accepted their...relationship, but maybe she couldn't accept the way he really felt about her. He knew beyond a doubt that he loved her. All the time and with all his heart, but he didn't think she'd want to hear it. Meeting each other's sexual needs was one thing. Loving each other—especially the way he loved her—was something else again.

The closest he came to telling her was an afternoon when she'd come in from work with Scottie in the car. The kid greeted him with another running hug, and they spent the rest of the daylight hours as a comfortable threesome on the patio. Kate worked on her pots of flowers, while he supervised and kept Scottie entertained.

And vice versa.

Scottie was a funny little kid, and Doyle enjoyed his take on the world around him.

"Do you like boys, Aunt Kate?" Scottie asked at one point, and Doyle nearly choked on his iced tea.

He looked at her, extremely interested in whatever her response was going to be to that inquiry.

"You mean the ones that are made out of snakes and snails and puppy dog tails?" she asked, trying not to grin.

"No," Scottie said. "I mean the ones that are me and Bugs."

The smile got away from her. "I especially like the ones that are you and Bugs," she said.

Doyle had come so close to saying it out loud then. Just out with it.

I love you, Kate.

He loved her so much it *hurt*. And all the while he felt like a man dancing on the edge of a precipice. Sometimes he could reach her, touch her, hold her. Sometimes he couldn't. But sooner or later he was going over the edge.

One hot afternoon when he was in the Bee Library, he caught a glimpse of someone coming up on the porch. At first he thought it was Arley but then changed his mind. Mrs. Bee was out, and he went hobbling to the door to see who it was and what she wanted.

He didn't see her when he reached the screen door. He opened it and stepped out onto the porch.

"Hey, good-lookin'," Rita said, ambushing him with a bear hug. "Look at you! Walking and everything!"

"Rita—" he said, completely taken by surprise. "I didn't know you were back."

"Sure you did." She grinned mischievously and moved to sit on the porch swing, pulling her long legs up under her. "You've just had other things on your mind—or so I hear."

He didn't say anything. He was still assessing his reaction to her sudden appearance. He was glad to see her. And he still thought she was beautiful—but it wasn't the same. She was his friend, one he would always care about and help if need be—but there wasn't anything more.

"So how's married life?" he asked, hobbling over to the swing to sit beside her.

"Great! Better than great!"

She waited until he'd sat down to grill him. "Well, tell me! What is this I hear about you and Meehan?"

"Who told you about that?"

"Who told me? *Everybody* told me—and quit dodging the question. Is it serious?"

He didn't quite know how to answer. *He* was serious.

"Got it that bad, huh?" Rita said.

"Yeah," he said after a moment.

"Does she know it?"

"Nah."

"You going to tell her?"

"I doubt it."

"Why not!"

"I don't want to scare her off," he said truthfully.

"Not telling her might scare her off, too. If you love her, you ought to tell her, Bugs."

He didn't say anything.

"*Do* you love her?"

"Looks like it," he said, then grinned. "That's not for publication," he added, and she smiled.

"I'm happy for you, Bugsy. But don't waste time here, okay? Look at all the time Mac and I wasted. When I think of how close we came to losing everything—well, you know. You were there."

"Yeah," he said. "I was there."

She looked at her watch. "Speaking of time, I'd better go pick up Mac before the traffic gets all backed up on the boulevard. I just wanted to drop by and see how you were doing for myself. Love agrees with you, mister."

"You, too," he said.

She laughed in that way she had and ran lightly down the steps to her car, turning once to give him a little wave. He watched her drive off, trying to decide if he felt better now that he'd admitted his feelings for Kate to someone.

Yeah, he decided. He did.

He sat on the porch for a while, expecting Kate to come home from work at her usual time. She didn't, and eventually he decided to go back inside and up to his apartment.

The phone rang when he was halfway up the stairs. With some difficulty he managed to backtrack and answer it.

"Hey," Kate said, and he smiled broadly.

"Hey, yourself. You're running late. All hell break loose...again?"

He could hear her give a little sigh. "Yes. But I'm on my way home in a few minutes, I think. I...want you to give me about forty-five minutes after I get there—before you come over."

"Okay.... Why?"

"You'll see," she said. "See you later."

He stood there holding the receiver after she'd hung up, still smiling.

Whatever it was, it sounded promising.

Very promising.

It was almost dark by the time she pulled into the drive and completely dark by the time the forty-five minutes were up. It was also going to rain—the fireflies were hovering close to the ground—one of Pop Doyle's no-fail indicators of a soon-to-happen evening thundershower.

The first drops began to fall when he was halfway across the yard, and he savored the smell of rain on hot, dusty ground. By the time he reached the hedges, it was coming down hard. He glanced at the stone bench as he passed it, thinking of the day Kate had been sitting there and Mrs. Bee had all but shoved him out the door to go riding to the rescue.

Rain or no rain he couldn't walk fast, then or now, and he could barely see where he was going. The house was dark except for a dim light coming, he thought, from the den or the hall. He rapped lightly on the back door, and when she didn't come, he opened it and went inside.

He could hear soft music playing somewhere in the house. Some kind of stringed instrument. A Celtic harp, maybe, or a dobro.

Haunting.

Melancholy.

A lighted candle burned on the mantel in the den. He could just make out Scottie's picture in one of the silver frames. The candle flame wavered slightly as he walked past.

"Kate?" he said.

She still didn't answer, and he kept going.

He bypassed the kitchen and went down the hallway toward her bedroom. He could see a flicker of light coming from there.

He saw her when he reached the doorway. She was sitting on the side of the bed. There were more lighted candles—on the dresser and the nightstand. She stood up when she saw him, came to him, took him by the hand.

"What...?" he began, but she pressed her fingertips against his lips.

She led him into the room. He was drenched to the skin, and without prelude she began to dry him gently with a towel. Her fingers lightly caressed his face from time to time, lightly touched his mouth. When she was done, she began to undress him, still saying nothing. He couldn't keep from smiling. He had thought her invitation sounded promising, but this was way beyond that. She kept walking between him and the light from the candles. He could see her body through the thin gown-like thing she was wearing, and his breath caught. He wanted to touch her, but she eluded his grasp, still saying nothing. When he was naked, she took him by the hand again and led him to the bed—no, to the place she had made for him there.

He lay down where she wanted, his back resting against a number of pillows placed against the headboard.

He started to say something again, then didn't. He gave himself up to whatever this was instead, closing his eyes after a moment.

Waiting.

The music played softly. It had that echo sound, he realized, sort of like the song he and Kate had danced to after Mrs. Bee's anniversary dinner.

The rain fell.

He could feel her come onto the bed and kneel beside him. He opened his eyes when she took his hand. She touched it lovingly, caressing it, running her fingers gently between his. When she pressed her warm lips into his palm, he gave a small gasp at the unexpected intensity of his response.

She moved closer to him.

"Close your eyes," she whispered, and when he didn't, she leaned over him to kiss his eyelids closed, first one, then the other. And she didn't stop with that. She kissed his cheek softly, his forehead,

the other cheek, and finally the corner of his mouth.
His breath grew heavy, and his hands began to trem-
ble.

He wanted to touch her, needed to touch her.

"Kate—"

"Shhh. My fantasy," she said against his ear. Her
breasts lightly brushed against his chest. He could
feel her nipples, hard with desire, through the silky
cloth.

Her fingertips moved lightly over his shoulders,
down his arms and back, over his chest and down
his thighs, touching him everywhere.

Almost.

Her hands were warm and gentle. He had never
had this experience before, not even with her. She
had touched him before, of course, but not like this,
not with such...

Love was the only thing that came to mind.

Love.

Her hands became bolder. He was having a hard
time lying still. She moved to kiss his mouth, softly
at first, and then—

He looked into her eyes.

What is it?

He reached for her. He thought for a moment she
was going to cry.

"Kate..."

He tried to say more, but she wouldn't let him.
Her mouth covered his again, the kiss hungry,
needy. He returned it. Whatever he had, whatever

she wanted—his body, his soul, his last dime—it was hers.

He pulled the gown over her head, and she came to him. He wrapped his arms around her, and then he was inside her.

I love you, Kate!

The music played.

The rain fell.

He woke up alone. The house was quiet now. Quiet and dark. He sat up on the side of the bed and switched on the lamp. His clothes were folded and stacked on the foot of the bed. He reached for them—they were warm, as if they'd just come out of the dryer.

He thought he heard her talking, and he put them on in case the sisters were here for some reason, and made his way slowly down the hall to the kitchen. Kate was sitting in the dark at the kitchen table, talking to someone on the phone. There was just enough light for him to see that she was dressed and purposeful. It made him more than a little uneasy.

"Don't turn on the light," she said as he came through the doorway.

The phone call must have ended, because she put the phone down on the table.

"Are you...all right?" he asked, because she wouldn't let him ask that or anything else earlier.

"Yes," she said. He could hear her take a deep breath. "Sit down, okay?"

He pulled out a chair and sat down.

"Do you remember when I asked you once if you wanted the truth and you said, 'Always'?"

"I remember."

"I hope you meant it—because I want to tell you the truth now."

"Go ahead," he said, but a thousand alarm bells were going off in his head. He reached across the table to put his hand on hers. She took her hand away.

"I..."

"Go ahead," he said again when she didn't get any further.

"I care about you," she said after a moment.

He stared at her across the table. He'd heard *that* before and he knew exactly what it meant. He had no great expectations when it came to women. Never had. Never would. He was glad that it was dark. He didn't want to see the look in her eyes.

"Nobody has ever—"

"Could we just get to the bottom line here?" he interrupted.

"It's over," she said quietly, and he could feel the breath go out of him. "I thought I would be all right with this—with you and me—but I'm not."

He started to get up, to get away from what she was saying, but then he changed his mind, mostly because he felt as if he'd been kicked in the gut and he wasn't sure he could stand.

Sometimes you hit the ground. Sometimes the ground hits you.

He sat there, knowing he could make it hard for her, for them both. He could make her spell it out for him, make her justify her decision with reasons—or lies. But he didn't. It took every ounce of control he had to keep his voice sounding normal.

"Okay," he said.

"Cal…"

"I said okay. Whatever you want. Our being together—it's that kind of an arrangement, isn't it? No strings. No anything but bailing whenever somebody feels like it. You just happened to feel like it first." He stopped, hoping, praying that she would contradict him—tell him that he'd completely misunderstood, like she had the other time.

But she didn't. She didn't say a word, and the silence between them lengthened.

"So when did you know you'd had enough?" he asked in spite of everything he could do. "Last week? Today? Was it something I said or did?"

"No—"

He gave a sharp sigh. He had to get out here before he did something really stupid. "Well, that's good to know, I guess. So. That's it then."

"Cal…" she said again.

"What, Kate! If it's over, it's over!" He pushed the chair back and struggled to his feet. "I do have one question, though. If it's not too much trouble."

"What is it?"

"What the hell was that in there just now!" he asked, pointing toward the bedroom. "One for the road? Send the poor dumb jerk on his way happy? What?"

But even as he asked, he knew what it was. It was Kate Meehan, saying goodbye.

He was overbalanced and he crashed into the edge of the kitchen table.

"It's okay!" he said when she tried to help him. "*I'm* okay. You don't need to worry about me."

"Cal," she said when he reached the back door. He looked around at her, but he didn't wait to hear whatever else she had to say.

"Oh, yeah," he said. "I guess I'd better say thanks. Thanks a lot, Kate. I'll say one thing. You're the best I ever had."

Chapter Eleven

You can't make a woman love you if she doesn't.

He couldn't remember when he didn't know that little truth. He'd learned the hard way. It was seared into his brain somewhere in big capital letters. And it didn't help.

He couldn't sleep, didn't really care if he ate, and what little energy he had he used trying to stay out of Mrs. Bee's way and off the church ladies' radar. The most positive thing he'd done in the past few days was to let the cat in and out.

He kept going over and over everything in his mind. What Kate said. What he said. And what he *should* have said.

Why the hell didn't I see this coming?

That was the question that dogged him so. He hadn't had this problem with Rita, so why hadn't he sensed that Kate was on her way out the door? It wasn't like he hadn't been on the qui vive—as his old drill sergeant used to say. He had been, but there was no point in pretending that he hadn't been completely knocked over by Kate's invitation to run along. He still didn't understand how he could have been so dense. He'd never mistaken Rita's feelings for him as anything but friendship. Kate was a friend, too, as far as that went—but there was more. There had *always* been more. He knew that, damn it. He'd felt it, even before they had become lovers.

He realized how hard it was for her to come to terms with their being together. He knew that the sisters were afraid that her association with him meant that she was going into some kind of emotional tailspin because the real estate guy had dumped her—the same way she had when her husband blew off their marriage. She might have been afraid of that herself, but he'd thought that at least for the time being she had resolved the misgivings she'd had.

Clearly, he'd thought wrong, because here he sat staring at the walls, while she—he didn't know what the hell she was doing.

He gave a heavy sigh. One thing for sure—he was going to have to find another place to live. He didn't think he could stand seeing her every day. Or not seeing her every day. So far, he'd managed not to hang out the window trying to spot some movement over at her place, but it hadn't been easy. Nothing about this was easy. He couldn't stop remembering the way she looked and felt...tasted...

Damn.

He kept thinking about making love with her, especially the last time—*her* fantasy, she said. Well, it was some fantasy, he'd give her that. He'd always be glad he was on the receiving end of it, regardless of the grand finale when he got the boot, regardless of the way he felt now.

He was going to have to do something and soon—but for now he only had one thing on his list. Feeling sorry for himself.

No problem. Too easy.

He'd had all that practice right after Rita's wedding—and right before he fell totally in love with Kate Meehan.

Someone rapped sharply on his door. He ignored it.

Whoever it was knocked again. The knock was too heavy to be Mrs. Bee's, but he still made no effort to answer it. He sat there, willing it all to go away.

"Doyle!" someone said, knocking louder, and he closed his eyes, tuning everything out but the misery.

The knock came again—this time down low on the door.

He opened his eyes, wondering what the hell.

When the tentative, low knock came again, he struggled to get up and moving. He could hear two people talking in the hallway.

"We just knocked," he heard a male voice say.

When he opened the door, Arley, Scottie and a soldier whose name tag Doyle couldn't quite read stood in the hallway. Old habits died hard, and he looked to the vaguely familiar soldier first.

"I'm Priority Two," the soldier said, nodding discreetly in Scottie's direction—which indicated two things. His presence here wasn't official and he had at least some understanding of what it was like to be a little boy.

Doyle looked down. Scottie stood there, looking like he was on his way to the gallows, his bottom lip was trembling.

"Hey, Scottie—"

"Where's my sister?" Arley interrupted.

"I don't know," he said to her. "What's the matter, buddy?" he asked Scottie.

"I got in trouble, Bugs," the boy said.

"What kind of trouble, man?"

"The teacher was really, really *mad*."

"Where is my sister!" Arley asked again.

"I don't know, Arley. I haven't seen her."

"I don't believe you."

"Well, I can't help that—Scottie, what happened?"

"I hit…Wesley."

"Did he need hitting?"

"What kind of question is that?" Arley demanded, finally taking an interest in her son's difficulties.

"Look. Who came to whose door here? If you don't want him to talk to me about this, tell him."

She threw up both hands and gave him the floor.

"Why did you hit him, Scottie?" Doyle asked.

"He was…making…armpit…noises at me!"

Ah, yes, Doyle recalled, trying not to grin. Damned hard for a man to walk away from *those*.

The confession apparently was too much for Scottie, and he grabbed Doyle around the knees. Doyle had to hold on to the doorjamb to keep from toppling over, still fighting a grin in spite of his current misery and Arley's obvious impatience. It took him a few seconds to make sure he wasn't going to laugh.

"I guess he wouldn't stop, huh?" he said, reaching down to pat Scottie on the back.

"No! He just kept on and on!"

"Well, I tell you what. It's not good to go hitting people like that, even if they're asking for it. Teachers and mothers and sergeants—they don't like it."

"And aunts," Scottie said, trying not to cry.

"Them, too. Look up here at me." He waited until he could see the boy's unhappy face. "What you have to do is not let Wesley know he's getting to you. If you don't pay him any attention, he ends up looking like an idiot. Just be cool. Mr. Cool all the way, okay?"

"O…kay," Scottie said, his voice wavering.

"Outstanding." Doyle glanced at Arley to see if he could follow his own advice. She was looking at Priority Two. Priority Two was very careful not to look back.

Doyle took the opportunity to read his name tag. "Baron." The COC—Chain of Concern—soldier Kate had volunteered.

"See, Scottie?" Arley said abruptly, reaching out to pat her son on the head. "That's what I said. Just don't pay any attention to Wesley."

Scottie let go of the choke hold he had on Doyle's knees. "Mr. Cool!" he said, clearly feeling better.

"Doyle, are you going to help me or not?" Arley asked.

"Arley, I don't know where Kate is."

"Well, *I* don't, either," she said, as if that was all his fault. "She's not at work and she's not at home and nobody's talked to her."

"I have," Priority Two said, and they both looked at him. "If you're talking about Kate Meehan."

"When?" Doyle asked, sounding more like Arley than he cared to admit.

"A couple of hours ago—she sent me over here."

"Why would she do that?"

"Well, she said she thought you wouldn't get to your clinic appointment—and you definitely needed to keep it."

"I know that," Doyle said. Which was the truth. He hadn't forgotten the appointment. He simply planned to ignore it. "When did you say you talked to her?"

"A couple of hours ago—at the hospital."

"They told *me* she wasn't working today," Arley said.

"She wasn't. She just came by the unit for something."

"For what?" Doyle and Arley said in unison. The now wary Baron kept looking from one of them to the other.

"She...didn't say. She just wanted to make sure Doyle got to his appointment—make sure he remembered—make sure he had a ride. She didn't mention what to tell a sister at all," he said to Arley. "Sorry."

"Well, you people are just no help whatsoever," Arley said. "Come on, Scottie. Mrs. Bee said she'd find a cookie for you."

"'Bye, Bugs," the boy said, trotting off with his mother.

"Yeah, wild man. You take it easy."

Doyle stood there, staring into space, trying to assess this latest development—until Baron gave a discreet cough.

"What the hell do you want?" Doyle asked him.

"Cut me some slack, man. I'm just trying to get you where you're supposed to be."

"I don't need any help."

"Kate said you'd probably give me grief. And if you did, she wanted me to tell you one thing."

Doyle stood waiting to hear what the "one thing" was—but the SOB was going to make him ask for it.

"Okay, what is it?" he said after a moment.

"She said, 'Please.'"

"And?"

"And nothing. 'Please.' That was it."

Doyle stared at him.

Please.

The one word that would get to him. He gave a sharp sigh.

"So are we going or not?" Baron asked, looking at his watch. "You've got fifteen minutes. If I drive like a bat out of hell, I can get you there."

"Yeah, like a doctor was ever on time in this man's army."

"Does that mean you're going?"

"I'm going, I'm going."

"Outstanding," Baron said, taking the liberty of pulling the apartment door closed. "So is she married?"

"Who?" Doyle asked, still out of sorts. He had no idea what Kate was doing. He didn't even have a clue. She dumps him...but she's worried about him keeping his appointments. As she'd said once herself—

This is insane.

And the really insane part was that the rest of the Meehan girls didn't know what was going on with her, either.

"The sister—Arley," Baron said. "Is she married?"

"Do I look like a hook-up service?" Doyle said sarcastically.

"No, you look like hell—but who's going to notice with that sunny disposition?"

"How did you get roped into this, anyway?" Doyle asked him as he hobbled out onto the porch.

"Damned if I know. Story of my life, though."

For once the army doctor was on time. Doyle barely made it into the waiting area before his name was called. This doctor he knew. His name was Julius, and he'd done a number of Doyle's surgeries.

"Damn," Julius said in the hallway. "What happened to you?"

"Sir?" Doyle said, thinking maybe Baron hadn't exaggerated when he said he looked like hell.

"Last time I saw you you could barely stand and you must have had a half a dozen dummy cords hooked to you so you wouldn't lose everything you dropped."

"Sir, I've been walking a lot."

Among other things.

"Doing the physical therapy exercises they taught you?"

"Sir, yes, sir."

Also among other things.

"And if you drop something on the floor, you can get it now?"

"Sir, yes, sir. No dummy cords, sir."

"Good. Of course, this is going to tick off a certain hot-shot Texas orthopedic surgeon."

"Sir?"

"You might as well know he and I had a difference of opinion about your rehabilitation."

Doyle didn't say anything.

"He did tell you he wanted to do surgery again."

"Sir, yes, sir."

"What do you think about that?"

"I think I'd rather burn in, sir," Doyle said, using the term for a paratrooper's fate when his chute didn't open.

Julius laughed—when Doyle wasn't particularly making a joke.

"Well, let's don't do that, okay? We might not get you put back together this time. How much pain are you having?"

"I'm not taking anything for it, sir."

"That's not exactly what I asked, but we'll let it go. I want to get another film or two today—just to make sure there isn't anything new going on. If it looks okay, I'm going to say you've dodged the bullet for the time being—and you can go in peace. For three months—unless you start having trouble. You know the drill by now. Keep walking. Keep exercising. Keep doing whatever you've been doing."

"Sir, yes sir."

I wish.

"All right then. Dismissed."

Kate, Kate.

She'd been determined that he get here to talk to the surgeon who wasn't all that gung-ho about dashing into the operating room. The news was good—excellent—and she'd gone out of her way to make sure he got it.

But he was no closer to understanding her than he'd been the other night. He stood for a moment in the hallway before he made up his mind about what he wanted to do. Then, with a sense of purpose he hadn't felt in some time, he headed for the floor where Kate worked. Plan A was to see if he couldn't get something from one of her co-workers about where she was. He didn't see anyone anywhere when he stepped off the elevator, but then he spotted a medic in a supply closet, counting bottles and boxes.

Baron.

"I want to ask you something," Doyle said when he looked up from the clipboard.

"What?"

"Do you have any idea where Kate is?"

"Me? No."

"She didn't say anything besides what you told me."

"No," Baron said, going back to counting small white boxes.

"Are you sure?"

"I'm sure."

"Look, Baron, it's important. I'm—" He

stopped, trying to decide how candid he wanted to be. He took a deep breath. "I'm worried about her, man. So is her sister. You saw that. Kate's important to me. If you know anything—anything at all, tell me."

Baron stopped counting, but he didn't say anything.

"Are you going to help me out or not?" Doyle asked.

"I don't really know anything to tell you... except—"

"Except what?" Doyle asked, trying to keep the desperation out of his voice.

"It's just something I overheard one of the nurses say."

"What?"

"Something about Kate having to go get a repeat X-ray last Friday."

Doyle felt the wind go out of him. "And?"

"That's it."

"What kind of X-ray?"

"I don't know. That's all I heard. It may not mean anything..."

"Yeah. Okay. Thanks," Doyle said absently.

But he was afraid he knew exactly what it meant.

"Mrs. Bee!" he yelled as soon as he cleared the screen door. Mrs. Bee came hurrying out of the kitchen, her hand resting on her chest.

"Calvin, you scared me!"

"Sorry, Mrs. Bee. I need to ask you something. Do you have any idea where Kate is?"

"No, Calvin. I haven't seen her."

"If you wanted to find her, where would you look?"

Mrs. Bee stood staring at him with her school-teacher face on, and all he could do was tough it out.

"Is something wrong, Calvin?"

"Yeah. I need to talk to her." He braced himself for the third degree, but thankfully Mrs. Bee didn't ask him anything. He could just hear himself trying to explain that Kate had dumped him, that she'd made him keep his clinic appointment and she'd had a repeat X-ray—so he had to find her.

"Well, I'd start with the sisters," Mrs. Bee said after a moment.

"Arley says they don't know where Kate is."

"Well, *she* might not."

"Meaning?"

"Meaning it might be better to start with the weakest link."

"I don't know what that means, Mrs. Bee."

"It means I can call Gwen…if you want me to."

"Yeah, Mrs. Bee. That would be great."

"All right. Let's see what Gwen says. And don't cramp my style. I work better alone."

He couldn't help but smile. "Okay, Mrs. Bee."

He waited in the kitchen while she made the call.

It took a while. The link must not have been as weak as Mrs. Bee thought.

"Did you find out anything? What did she say?" he asked, pouncing on the old lady as soon as he heard her hang up the receiver.

"I didn't find out where Kate is—but I did find out that Gwen knows."

"She knows? Are you sure?"

"I'm sure. When I asked her where Kate was, she sounded like Porky Pig."

"Porky Pig?"

"Exactly. I didn't teach school all those years not to know what *that* means."

Doyle looked at her, more than a little lost.

"Do you think you can drive Thelma and Louise, Calvin?" Mrs. Bee abruptly asked. "I think you should take my car and drive over to Gwen's and see if Katie is there. If she's not, maybe you can talk Gwen into telling her something for you. What do you think?"

What he thought was that the unexpected offer to turn him loose with Thelma and Louise came close to making him sound like Porky Pig, too.

"I think I can drive the car, Mrs. Bee—but are you sure you want to trust me with it?"

"I'm sure. It'll help your image."

"My image?"

"Katie knows what that car means to me. If she sees I let you drive it, she'll know somebody thinks you're worthy."

"Or she'll think I hog-tied you and took the keys," he said, and Mrs. Bee laughed and swatted the air.

"Now, let's see…where did I put those keys—oh, I know. I'll be right back. You be thinking about what you need to say to Katie while I go get them."

He had a lot of things he wanted to say, but there was only one thing that mattered.

I love you, Kate.

If he could just get that said and make her believe it, then maybe the rest of it would take care of itself.

Mrs. Bee came back with the keys and the directions to Gwen's house written on a sheet of pink notebook paper. "Good luck," she said when she handed them over.

He smiled suddenly. Some knights had white chargers. He had a vintage Thunderbird.

"Thanks, Mrs. Bee. You don't know how much I appreciate this."

"I think I do, Calvin."

"Well. Here goes nothing—keep your fingers crossed for me."

"I will."

"The church ladies, too."

"That goes without saying, Calvin."

He headed purposefully toward the back door, then stopped.

"Mrs. Bee? I want to ask you something."

"What is it, Calvin?"

"I want to ask you about Michael Mont. About why you told Kate I reminded you of that guy."

Mrs. Bee smiled. "Because God made you merry, Calvin. And no matter what happens, you still think life is worthwhile."

Mrs. Bee's vision of him caught him completely off guard. Did he think life was worthwhile? Maybe he did. He had his down moments, but thus far he supposed that he hadn't stayed down.

But he was on the verge of staying down now.

Kate!

If she was sick again...

He had to wait a minute before he trusted his voice enough to say anything.

"Thanks, Mrs. Bee," he said finally.

"Go find Katie," she said.

Chapter Twelve

He went on his quest with the top down and the radio blaring, letting the music get him pumped up and ready for the ordeal ahead.

"Never surrender..."

Hell, no!

"Lover...

Best friend...

In my heart, in my soul...."

He didn't have any problem finding the house; Mrs. Bee had given him good directions. It was still daylight when he got there, but just barely. He didn't see Kate's car anywhere, and he briefly considered abandoning the mission.

But only briefly. Her car could be around back or

in the garage. And even if she was there, there was no guarantee that she would talk to him. Either way, he might still have to concentrate on the "weakest link."

He pulled into the driveway and parked. It took him a little while to get out of the car. He'd managed the driving part, but getting out of those low seats was something else again.

He saw someone move aside the curtain in a front window as he hobbled up the curved sidewalk to the front door. The brick steps to the porch were steep and precarious, but he managed. He looked around before he rang the doorbell. It was nice out here— plants and an old-fashioned glider with big yellow-flowered cushions. It was the kind of place Kate would enjoy.

He rang the doorbell, and he imagined the emotional—if not physical—scramble his being here must be causing on the other side of the door. But right or wrong, he was here. This was it.

It took a while, but the front door finally opened.

"Cal!" Gwen said as if she were surprised. "What are you doing here!" From the look on her face, it was a question she regretted immediately. She had thrown the door wide open in more ways than one.

"Hey, Gwen. Can I talk to Kate?"

There was no point in dragging it out. He was going to work from the assumption that she was on the premises, and apparently he was right, because it took Gwen a long time to answer.

"I…well…it's—" She took a deep breath. "She doesn't want to see you, Cal."

"I just need to say a couple of things to her, and then I'll go. Can you ask her if she'll let me do that—let me say what I came to say?"

Gwen stood there, shifting from one foot to the other. He actually felt sorry for her. Clearly, go-between was not a job she relished.

"Please," he said, and she sighed.

"I'll ask her—but don't get your hopes up."

She closed the door. His legs were beginning to hurt, and he hobbled over to the glider and sat down.

And waited. It was a nice evening—less humid than usual—and there was a slight breeze. He could hear kids playing someplace nearby—skateboarding from the sound of it. He listened to them for a time, then to the squeak of the glider as he moved it back and forth.

He closed his eyes, trying to take Mrs. Bee's earlier advice and figure out what he was going to say. The front door opened again, and Kate stepped out. Whatever speech he might have had in place completely dissipated.

He couldn't stop looking at her. She had on some kind of long cotton dress with a slit up the side—some kind of beach or poolside thing. Her hair was loose and hanging to her shoulders. She brushed it away from her face, but not so she could see him better. He hadn't realized that seeing her under these circumstances would hurt so much.

Ah, Kate.

"Nice wheels," she said after a moment, but she wouldn't look at him.

He smiled. "I guess you know where I got them. I...saw Julius today. The surgery's off—for a while, anyway. But I guess you know that, too."

She nodded absently and looked across the front yard toward the street. A car with a window-rattling speaker system went by.

"Gwen said you needed to talk to me," she said after the car had passed, putting an end to the pleasantries she'd initiated.

"Are you okay?" he asked, because she was determined to avoid any eye contact, and he couldn't tell.

She ignored the question.

"I want to know if you're all right, Kate!"

She looked at him then; he could feel the effort it took for her to do it. "I don't know," she said. She gave a small shrug. "I haven't heard from the biopsy yet."

Oh, damn! Damn it!

He realized that she must be working from her own assumption—that she thought his coming here like this must mean that he somehow knew what was going on with her. And she meant to derail him with the unadulterated truth. He understood that immediately. But it wasn't going to work. He wasn't the real estate guy.

He kept looking at her, trying to hold it together. It was every bit as bad as he had feared, and it was all he could do not to reach for her.

"I didn't wake up this morning thinking I wanted to make things worse for you," he said finally. "I know you don't want me here, so I'm just going to get it over with. All I want you to do is listen. I need to tell you this—because I'm not sure you understand how it is with me.

"See, I don't care what people think about you and me being together. I don't care about the age difference. I know how old you are, by the way. I was still a patient when they decorated the nurses' station with black crepe paper and had that big four-oh party for you.

"I also don't care that this thing started when both of us were on the rebound. I do care that maybe the cancer has come back. That worries the hell out of me—because I love you, Kate. That's it. That's what I wanted to tell you. Whether you like it or not. Whether it's right or wrong or convenient. It doesn't matter. I *love* you. Big joke, huh?

"It really hurt when you broke it off the way you did—but as bad as that was, it's nothing compared to what I'm feeling right this minute—because I only just realized what you really think of me. See, I thought we were up front with each other. I thought you cared about me and you even trusted me a little. I thought there was more to us than just a good roll in the hay. But I was wrong about all that.''

''Cal—''

''I don't understand why you couldn't tell me what was happening with you! Did you think I was too dumb to get how scared you must be? I know how scared you are, Kate. I'm scared, too. I don't want anything to happen to you. I'm arrogant enough to think I might be able to help you through this stuff—and that's because it was always easier for me when I wasn't doing so good if *you* were around. Two-way street, you know?

''That night when Mrs. Bee got you out of the shower and made you come see about me. You said something about me forgiving myself. I thought you were going to say everything happens for a reason— and it made me mad, because I couldn't see a reason for me to make it when the others died.

''But now I'm thinking maybe there is a reason. Maybe I made it so I'd be here for *you.* How do you like that for arrogance, Kate?''

He was making her cry—the last thing in this world he wanted to do. She wiped furtively at her eyes, but he didn't stop.

''I'm not like your sorry-assed ex-husband or any of the rest of them. I thought you knew that. It hurts so *bad,* Kate, knowing you don't want anything from me now when you're—'' He had to stop because his voice broke. He struggled to his feet.

''That's all I have to say—except that I hope everything turns out all right—the biopsy, I mean. I'm not going to make things worse for you. If you want me, you know where to find me.''

''Cal…this is *my* problem.''

''Right. Oh, you might want to call Arley. I know she's not authorized to be affected by this thing, either, but she's pretty worried about what's going on with you—in an Arley sort of way.''

He didn't wait for her to say anything else. He dragged himself to the car and he didn't even remember the trip. He was barreling down the highway in Thelma and Louise somehow, and he didn't look back. Not once. He couldn't—not if he intended to leave her. He *had* to leave her. She didn't want him around. What else could he do?

Mrs. Bee was waiting up for him. She took one look at him, and the hopeful expression on her face died.

''I put Thelma and Louise back in the shed,'' he said, avoiding her eyes. ''I don't think I broke anything.''

She didn't say anything until he was halfway up the stairs.

''Calvin?''

He stopped, but he didn't turn around. ''I gave it my best shot, Mrs. Bee.''

''I know you did.… Calvin?''

He gave a quiet sigh. ''Yeah, Mrs. Bee?''

''You're a good boy, Calvin.''

Oh, yeah, he thought. Him and Michael Mont. He hadn't read the whole book, so he didn't know how things worked out for the guy. Not good, he supposed. Those big, thick books with the jackets still on them were too much like real life.

He was *tired*. Too tired to even think anymore. It was all he could do to drag the rest of the way up the stairs. The cat came from somewhere and dogged his heels down the hallway.

In spite of his fatigue, he showered and fixed himself a tomato and cheese sandwich. He even managed to feed the cat before it got all the way to Act III of *The Cat from Hunger Dies*.

Then he sat down in front of the television, but he didn't turn it on. He just stared at it. What he needed was musical accompaniment for his misery—and he felt too bad to even pick up his guitar. He turned on the radio instead and searched for something in keeping with his mood. He finally settled on a tearjerker by one of the boy bands. Boy bands knew all about being big losers in the love department. He'd let them do his suffering for him, because they did it so well.

The cat jumped up on the chair arm and kept trying to lean on him.

"Beat it, tuna breath," he said.

But cats weren't put on this earth to follow orders, and it eventually settled itself against his side. He could feel it purring. He tried not to think of the day he'd gone to shoo Kate in out of the rain.

It seemed like a hundred years ago.

Another memory popped into his mind—Mrs. Bee talking about her first husband and the song he'd sung about the soldier praying for angels to protect the woman he loves. He had no problem getting with that.

Please, he thought. *Just let her be okay. That's all I ask. Please!*

When he was pretty sure he'd fall asleep if he hit the sack, he moved to the bedroom. Sleep came easily enough, but it didn't last. He woke with a start, thinking that the cat must be on midnight patrol again and had knocked something over. He raised up, trying to see.

Kate stood in the doorway.

At first, he wasn't sure if he was dreaming or not. The room was dark. He couldn't see her face. He heard her give a quiet sigh, but she still didn't say anything.

"So...did you come over the roof again?" he asked after a moment.

"Mrs. Bee let me in," she said, her voice sounding husky and strained.

"Are you going to stay over there...or are you coming over here?"

It was all the invitation she needed. She came to him then, lying down beside him. He held her tightly, stroking her face, her hair. He couldn't believe she was really here.

"You're going to have to help me out here," he said. "I don't want to jump to the wrong conclu—"

She stopped him with a kiss.

"Hold me," she said, clinging to him in the darkness. "Hold me—" She stopped abruptly. He thought she was crying.

He tightened his arms around her. "Kate—"

"You were...right. I am scared. I'm so scared I don't know what I'm doing. I'm...I hurt you. I didn't mean—"

She was crying hard now, and he let her. She needed to do that, he thought.

"I didn't want to...drag you...into this," she said. "You know...how you are."

"No. How am I?"

"You're...*loyal.*"

"And that's a bad thing, I guess."

"I didn't want you to feel obligated...to stick by me...because I...know you. You'd stay...no matter how you felt...about it. I care about you. The least I could do was give you a—"

"A what? A way out?"

"Yes!"

"Kate, *I'm* supposed to be the one to decide whether or not I want to bail. You didn't give me the chance."

"I know. I couldn't. I didn't—"

She gave a wavering sigh and pressed her face into his shoulder.

"Didn't what?" he asked after a moment.

"I didn't want to take the chance—that I might be wrong about you, too."

He gave a quiet sigh and held her closer.

Amazing, he thought. Sometimes women made perfect sense—once a man understood the particulars. Getting the particulars out of them was hell, though. Definitely, *definitely* hell.

"Don't do it again," he said. "Don't make decisions for me. Okay?"

"Okay," she said.

"I mean it."

"I know."

"Okay, then. Whatever happens, we're going to get through it. You and me. And the sisters and Mrs. Bee and the church ladies—and whoever the hell else it takes. I love you, Kate—more than I can ever tell you."

"I love you, too."

"Yeah?"

"Yeah."

"Tell me again."

"I love you, Cal."

He couldn't stop smiling—and he couldn't keep from fishing, either. "So…when did it happen? The 'love' thing."

"When you came out into the rain to see about me," she said.

"Damn, Kate!" he said, just as taken aback as he'd been when she told Mrs. Bee she had him chained to her bed. He kissed her. Hard. And held her close to him.

Women.

No. *This* woman.

He never would have guessed—not in a million years. He closed his eyes and savored his joy, pushing aside all the worry about what might be ahead for them. For now he would rely on the training he'd gotten from the military and from Pop Doyle—first things first and one step at a time.

Kate Meehan loved him. And that was all that mattered.

Epilogue

It was standing room only in Uncle Patrick's pub—friends and family—and strangers off the street. Doyle looked out across the sea of faces. Nina and his mother were conspicuously absent—he hadn't expected them to come—but the people who had managed to get there were all waiting for him to do something entertaining.

"So will you sing for us, Cal?" Uncle Patrick called from the bar.

"You're going to be sorry you asked that," he answered, making the crowd laugh.

"Should I be hidin' the tomatoes then, Cal?"

"I wish you would," he assured him. "But since

you did ask, I'm going to do it. Not too long ago somebody told me a story. It was a love story, and it was about a soldier—a paratrooper—'' He had to stop for the barks and whistles that came from the military presence in the crowd.

"This soldier went to war, and he didn't come home again. But before he left to go overseas, he sang a song to the woman he loved...in a place something like this one. It took me a while to find the words, but I did. And she's here tonight, helping us celebrate, so I'm going to sing it for her.''

He waited for the applause to die down.

"I'm going to sing it for her,'' he said again, "and I'm going to sing it for the woman *I* love. They're both sitting right over there—Mrs. Bee and my darling Kate.'' He could see Kate smile, and Mrs. Bee and the church ladies go all atwitter. "Clive and Jeffrey here are going to help me out with the music,'' he added.

Both musicians gave a little bow.

"When was it you got married?'' Clive asked him loudly enough for the back of the room to hear.

"Ah...two hours ago,'' Doyle said, knowing something was coming.

"Aha! Two hours ago, is it?'' Clive asked innocently.

"Right.''

"So this would be your *weddin'* night, would it?''

"It would.''

"Saints preserve us, boy, and you're wasting time up here *singin'!*"

"I'm going to sing fast," Doyle said above the laughter.

"Well, I should *hope* so!" Clive said, giving him a pointed look—and then another one in case the crowd missed the first one. Then he stepped back and began the melancholy intro on his fiddle, going through it twice until the room quieted down.

Doyle stood where he could see Kate's beautiful face.

He began to sing the words, and everything else fell away. There was no one here but her. She was well and safe now, and he adored her, his beautiful, beautiful wife.

He took her through the song with all the emotion his Irish roots could muster—through the soldier's long search for the one woman in this world that was his and his alone, his joy at finding her at last and his love and his prayers for her. He sang his heart out, and when he was done, like the time Bud Gaffney had sung it so long ago, there wasn't a dry eye in the house.

There was a moment of silence when the music ended, then the room exploded with applause. He shook hands with Clive and Jeffrey and stepped down from the stage. He walked to Mrs. Bee first, giving her a little bow and kissing her hand.

He turned to Kate and took her into his arms. She was crying. He kissed her, then kissed her again.

"I love you, Mrs. Doyle," he said. "Let's go home."

* * * * *

*If you'd like to read
more stories from
three-time Rita Award winner
Cheryl Reavis,
we hope you'll keep an eye out
for her next historical romance
THE BRIDE FAIR
coming in April 2002
from Harlequin Historicals.*

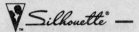
Silhouette® —
where love comes alive—online...

eHARLEQUIN.com

buy books

- ♥ Find all the new Silhouette releases at everyday great discounts.

- ♥ Try before you buy! Read an excerpt from the latest Silhouette novels.

- ♥ Write an online review and share your thoughts with others.

online reads

- ♥ Read our Internet exclusive daily and weekly online serials, or vote in our interactive novel.

- ♥ Talk to other readers about your favorite novels in our Reading Groups.

- ♥ Take our Choose-a-Book quiz to find the series that matches you!

authors

- ♥ Find out interesting tidbits and details about your favorite authors' lives, interests and writing habits.

- ♥ Ever dreamed of being an author? Enter our Writing Round Robin. The Winning Chapter will be published online! Or review our writing guidelines for submitting your novel.

All this and more available at
www.eHarlequin.com

SINTB1R2

Award-winning author
SHARON DE VITA
brings her special brand of romance to

SPECIAL EDITION™
and

SILHOUETTE *Romance*™

in her new cross-line miniseries

SADDLE

This small Western town was rocked by scandal when the youngest son of the prominent Ryan family was kidnapped. Watch as clues about the mysterious disappearance are unveiled—and meet the sexy Ryan brothers...along with the women destined to lasso their hearts.

FALLS

Don't miss:

WITH FAMILY IN MIND
February 2002, Silhouette Special Edition #1450

ANYTHING FOR HER FAMILY
March 2002, Silhouette Romance #1580

A FAMILY TO BE
April 2002, Silhouette Romance #1586

A FAMILY TO COME HOME TO
May 2002, Silhouette Special Edition #1468

Available at your favorite retail outlet.

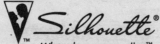

Where love comes alive™

Visit Silhouette at www.eHarlequin.com

SSERSFR